Love is
a time of enchantment:
in it all days are fair and all fields
green. Youth is blest by it,
old age made benign:
the eyes of love see
roses blooming in December,
and sunshine through rain. Verily
is the time of true-love
a time of enchantment — and
Oh! how eager is woman
to be bewitched!

# COUNTERFEIT COUNTESS

Rowan Winter had no intention of accepting Carl von Holstein's offer of a position with his cousin's children in the castle with the somewhat alarming name of Drachenschloss. To her amazement, Captain von Holstein was prepared to go to inordinate lengths to procure a governess, and before long she found herself aboard his yacht, accompanying him to Germany very much against her will. The true reason behind her abduction was revealed, and soon Rowan found herself living the life of a Countess!

*Books by Janis Coles*
*in the Ulverscroft Large Print Series:*

JANIS COLES

# COUNTERFEIT COUNTESS

*Complete and Unabridged*

**ULVERSCROFT**
*Leicester*

First published in Great Britain

First Large Print Edition
published 1996

British Library CIP Data

Coles, Janis
    Counterfeit Countess.—Large print ed.—
Ulverscroft large print series: romance
I. Title
823.914 [F]


ISBN 0–7089–3481–1

Published by
F. A. Thorpe (Publishing) Ltd.
Anstey, Leicestershire

Set by Words & Graphics Ltd.
Anstey, Leicestershire
Printed and bound in Great Britain by
T. J. Press (Padstow) Ltd., Padstow, Cornwall

This book is printed on acid-free paper

# 1

THE day was hot even for the time of year and Rowan felt uncomfortably warm under the prim white blouse she wore. The high bones in the collar dug into her neck and she envied the cool lace gowns of the fashionable ladies milling over the smooth lawns at Hillington House. Near at hand a band was playing a tune from the latest musical show, one that was known to be a particular favourite of the Prince of Wales. His Royal Highness had been due half an hour ago, everyone was awaiting his arrival with hidden anticipation.

Rowan's hands were firmly clasping two smaller, hotter ones and she looked down, somewhat wearily at her two charges, whom she had received a while ago pristine from their nurse's hands, and who had sadly wilted in the interval. Now, their white, starched skirts hung limp above pink knees, and the trim straw hats perched above hot flushed faces.

"Oh, Miss Winter," wailed the larger girl, "can't we go into the shade?"

"Want to go the river," cried her smaller sister, her lower lip beginning to pout ominously.

"So you shall, my pet," Rowan hastened to assure her, "but first we must wait until the Prince arrives and make our curtsys to him."

"He's late," announced Rose with satisfaction. "I expect he's not coming."

"Oh, course he's coming — and the Princess too — "

"Want to paddle," said Daisy, not to be diverted by the prospect of the august visitors. She kicked at the grass with the toe of one shoe and, pleased with the resulting green stain, tried to twist her hand free from the firm grip of her governess as she bent over, the better to admire it.

"Stand up, do," admonished her sister, "people can see your drawers."

"They've got lace on," Daisy told her, bending farther so that the brim of her hat almost touched the grass.

2

"If you're good, you can have strawberries for tea," Rowan offered, resorting to bribery.

"And ice cream?" asked Daisy, her upside-down face assuming an alarming hue.

"And ice cream," agreed their governess, "But now stand up or I will tell Nurse you are to be put to bed with bread and milk for supper."

"There's Mama," Rose cried suddenly, "Doesn't she look pretty!"

Diverted, her younger sister hurriedly resumed an upright position and ignoring her governess's attempts to smooth her crumpled skirts, peered in the direction of Rose's pointing finger. "*Doesn't* she look pretty!" she repeated, not to be outdone.

"May we go and talk to her, Miss Winter?" asked the older girl, her voice unconsciously wishful.

"Well . . . ," Rowan hesitated, knowing that Lady Devonish would have no wish to be bothered by her offspring at such a time. At that moment Daisy broke away from her grasp and made for her mother as quickly as her stumpy little legs would carry her. "Oh dear," sighed Rowan starting forward, aware of what her charge's reception would be.

"We'd best go and remove the child," advised Rose, echoing her mother's words, which she had heard many times in her young life.

Looking down, Rowan found her eyes surprisingly shrewd and knowledgeable in the shade provided by her hat brim. "Mama will not like her skirt to be crumpled," she pointed out.

Hurrying forward, Rowan caught Daisy before she could clutch her mother's pale lace dress and, holding her firmly, faced her employer. "Lady Devonish, may I remove the children — it really is much too hot for them," she said firmly, well aware that her children's comfort would count for little with their mother, but hoping that the fact that the group around her had heard would sway her decision.

"Daisy, pray don't touch me," snapped her mother, before turning a sharp gaze on the governess. "His Highness asked especially to see them," she said. "As his loyal subjects they must learn that one does not refuse a royal request."

There was an underlying tone of triumph in her voice and, not for the first time, Rowan found herself wondering if there was any truth in the backstairs gossip that linked the name of her employer with that of the Prince.

At that moment a wave of excitement stirred the milling throng and Rowan knew that Their Highnesses had arrived. In the triumph of the moment all was forgotten save the delight of being given the accolade of a successful society hostess and Lady Devonish swept forward to welcome Prince Edward and his Princess.

Mindful of her duties, Rowan put a detaining hand on both the girls' shoulders, before giving them a quick inspection to make sure they were respectable.

"Remember to curtsy and call him Your Royal Highness and then sir," she said briefly, leading them forward.

"My little chicks!" cried Lady Devonish dramatically, seeing them hover on the edge of the crowd. "May I present my children, sir?"

"Delighted — delighted," rumbled the Prince, always pleased to meet a pretty female, whatever her age and bent to engage Rose and Daisy in conversation for a few minutes.

Calling forward one of the men in the group that surrounded him, he took something from him and dropped it with a roar of laughter into the girls' outstretched hands. Judging the interview at an end Rowan came forward to take the children back into her care and found herself the object of the Prince's scrutiny. Reading the sudden interest in his gaze, she dropped a blushing curtsy and hastily taking the children's hands would have taken refuge in the watching crowd, but at that moment Prince Edward spoke.

"What is your name, Fräulein?" he asked in German.

"Rowan Winter, Your Highness," she answered in the same language, aware that Lady Devonish was not pleased by the attention bestowed on her governess.

"Winter?" he repeated, giving the name a German pronunciation.

Rowan shook her head "No, sir, I am English."

"But you speak German."

"It is often required in a governess, sir."

"You speak it very well." For a moment longer the pale, protuberant eyes studied her, leaving her with the uncomfortable feeling that for some reason she interested the Prince more than he was prepared to admit. "Your little flowers will grow up with an excellent accent," he said jocularly, turning to his hostess.

Once more his gaze swept over Rowan, a hint of speculation in his eyes before nodding pleasantly to the people gathered round he passed on, allowing his hostess to lead him to a striped awning, where tea awaited the royal party.

"He gave me a golden penny," Daisy announced with great satisfaction, opening a plump hand to display her treasure, sticking to her hot little palm.

"A half sovereign," corrected her elder sister knowledgeably. "Must we wait for the Princess, Miss Winter?"

Rowan peered about, standing on tiptoe in an attempt to see if Princess Alexandra was in the vicinity. "I — think not," she decided at last, unable to see an excited group which would proclaim the presence of the Princess. "Let us slip away before anyone notices us," and suiting the words to actions, seized her charge's hands and began to edge quietly away among the dispersing throng who were eager to follow in His Highness's footsteps and catch another glimpse of his exalted person.

Familiar with the paths and idiosyncrasies of the grounds, Rowan led the girls away from the crowds and, passing the kitchens, gathered up a waiting tray and continued on her way to the quiet of the nearby riverbank.

"Now we can relax," she declared, setting down her burden and seating herself on the cool grass. "No one saw us leave and we are quite alone."

"I fear you are mistaken, dear Miss Winter," Rose told her, surprisingly, "for that soldier has followed us. Do you think he can be a Prince, for he looks just like one from a fairytale."

Following her pointing finger, Rowan's eyes widened at the approaching figure. Tall and blond, resplendent in a blue-and-white Hussars uniform, he was so devastatingly handsome that she could quite see why Rose had supposed him a fairybook prince.

Clicking his heels smartly, he bowed his head a fraction and stared down his aquiline nose, his grey eyes shadowed by a peak of the tall, blue shako.

"Carl Von Holstein," he announced with only the slightest of accents. "Captain in His Imperial Majesty's Hussars."

Rowan lifted her eyebrows and waited for him to go on, somewhat puzzled by his behaviour; even in those modern times a gentleman did not usually introduce himself to an unknown lady and, judging by his manner, she would have thought that the aristocratic German before her was bound by etiquette. It occurred to her that, recognising her as a mere governess, he was set upon a flirtation with a member of the lower orders and instinctively her chin rose.

Seeing her action his gaze sharpened a little. "You are right in thinking I am taking advantage of your position," he said. "If you were not — what you are, I would not have felt at liberty to approach you." His eyes travelled over her, taking in the blouse and skirt she wore, which while the conventional garb of a governess, yet had an undeniable air of elegance and good taste. His eyes lingered on her face and hair, examining and scrutinising coldly, with none of the warmth and familiarity she had come to recognise in the amorous glances of Lady Devonish's friends.

"A little lower — and you would not have been suitable. A little higher — and you would have been out of reach."

Something about the encounter disturbed her and, suddenly making up her mind, Rowan turned to the two girls who had wandered down to the shallow river bank. "Daisy — Rose," she called sharply. "Come here, quickly. We must go back to the house."

A hand caught her wrist, moving almost lazily, but feeling surprisingly strong.

"Stay where you are, girls. You may have a little while longer to play," said the man and to her chagrin the children obeyed him readily, turning back to their game after the most cursory glance in her direction.

"How dare you!" she gasped. "Release

me at once, or I will shout for help."

"Who would hear you, Miss Winter?" He smiled at her start of surprise. "Oh, yes, I know your name. I only had to ask one of Lady Devonish's friends. They all know the charming, but distant Miss Winter."

"What do you want?" she demanded, having discovered that it was useless to try to free her wrist.

For answer, he tucked her hand under his elbow and held it there firmly, constraining her to turn and walk with him along the bank.

"Calm yourself, Fräulein, I am not about to abduct you or force my attentions upon you — I merely wish to place a proposition before you."

Rowan waited warily, her heart beginning to thud a little; after all the handsome stranger was very much bigger than she, his lithe movements speaking of strength and vigour, while he carried himself with an air of arrogance that filled her with unease. Ruthlessness and pride were written very clearly across his face, neither of which attributes pleased her or set her mind at ease.

"My cousin, Count Von Holstein, has need of a governess to take charge of his children. He has charged me with the task of finding a suitable female. You, Miss Winter, appear to fit the requirements excellently. I know you speak German . . . and obviously your credentials are of the highest order or Lady Devonish would not employ you."

Rowan stared at him, "Are you offering me the position?" she asked.

He sighed impatiently, "I am not propositioning you, Fräulein," he told her, "Whatever Lady Devonish is paying you, my cousin will double it."

Rowan gasped and at once an instinctive warning sounded in her brain. "There are agencies for governesses, you know," she pointed out, while puzzling over the situation in which she found herself.

"I am short of time — besides you are the one to suit; there is no need to look further."

"I am not available . . . I can't just leave. I am fond of the children — besides, Lady Devonish would never agree to it."

Carl Holstein turned her to face him.

"Then say nothing. Pack your things and I'll have a carriage waiting for you at the gate." He spoke with a particular intensity, leaning forward to hold her gaze with his light eyes. "I promise it will be worth your while."

Instinctively drawing back, Rowan saw with relief a group of people approaching and shook her head. "No," she said decisively, "I must decline your offer, Captain Von Holstein."

His grip tightened as a gleam of anger appeared in his eyes, but at that moment he too became aware that they were no longer alone and, releasing her, he stepped back.

"I am sorry that you feel unable to accommodate the Count," he said formally. "If you should change your mind, I shall be at Lady Devonish's ball tomorrow night."

Rowan was unable to restrain a smile, "My dear Captain," she said, "you are mistaken if you believe that a governess will attend her employer's ball."

His eyes flickered over her, "We shall see, Fräulein," he said and clicking his heels together, saluted her briefly before turning and sauntering away.

Watching his retreating back, that held more than a hint of a swagger, Rowan found herself puzzled rather than frightened, although she had to admit that the encounter had a tinge of unease about it and, feeling a little disturbed, she went to join the children at their picnic, but the afternoon had lost its pleasure. A heavy haze had crept up unnoticed and now obscured the sun, and the day had grown hot and oppressive. Rose and Daisy had grown tired of the river and even the prospect of strawberries and ice cream could not make them other than fractious and difficult.

Daisy wriggled uncomfortably in her crumpled white dress and, denied the pleasure of paddling, contrived to fall into the shallow river, whereupon Rose took the opportunity of joining her and they both wallowed happily in the cool water, until Rowan waded in herself and removed them by force.

"You naughty pair," she scolded, half laughing at the appearance they presented, their once immaculate dresses, stained and muddy, their carefully curled hair hanging in wet elf-locks about their faces, while water dripped and trickled its way out of their clothes and shoes.

"I falled in," asserted Daisy, licking a trickle of water as it slithered past her mouth.

"I rescued her," announced her sister, with a saintly air.

"You are both telling stories," their governess told them roundly, "and should be punished. However," she went on as their faces fell, "as you have had a singularly boring afternoon, I'll overlook your behaviour this once. Now what shall we do — I'm nearly as wet as you."

The children eyed her hopefully and, having examined the solitude of the river bank about them, she gave them both a conspiratorial smile, "I do believe everyone is having tea — if you take off your clothes quickly and be very quiet I think you could have a quick game in the water."

Almost before she had finished speaking the girls were undoing buttons and tapes and pulling dresses and petticoats over their wet heads. Daisy took everything off and plunged into the water like a naked cherub, but, mindful of her advanced years, Rose elected to keep on her drawers and chemise.

"Ten minutes," warned Rowan and then was so tempted by the cool water that she removed her own wet shoes and stockings and, holding up her long skirt, stepped down the muddy bank to join them in the river.

The water about her legs and feet was an exquisite pleasure, taking her in memory back to her own childhood and, carried away by the unusual freedom, she allowed the children to play much longer than she intended, until at last she became aware of an approaching group of people.

"Quick, children," she urged, realising almost at once that it was too late; they had already been noticed and, to her horror, she recognised that the Prince himself was among the watchers, with Lady Devonish upon his arm.

"Miss Winter!" gasped her employer and appeared about to faint at the dreadful sight presented by her children and their governess. "Your Highness," she recovered her aplomb enough to say,

"I can only apologise for my girls — I can only assure you that such disgusting behaviour — "

A great roar of laughter burst from Prince Edward. "My dear Lady Devonish," he cried, "I have not seen such a delightful sight since my own children were that age. I only wish I could join them."

"Miss Winter, what *can* you be thinking of? Take the children to the house at once — I shall speak to you all this evening."

The Prince recognised the grim note in his hostess's voice and set himself to placate her. "Let me ask a little favour of you, Lady Devonish," he began as she turned her back on the scene. "So pretty a sight, so sweet and innocent, does not deserve punishment. Because you are a generous woman of the world I know you will let them all off without even a scold."

There was a faint but undeniable emphasis upon the word 'all' and Lady Devonish recognised the royal command behind the suggestion. Giving in at once, she smiled over her shoulder, at the culprits, "His Highness has interceded for you — we will say no more about the incident," and smiling under the royal approval, she gathered up her group with practised ease and swept them away from the shocking scene.

Hastily scrambling up the bank, Rowan caught up her erring charges, pulled damp clothes over their heads and hurried them back to the house, wondering how she could have so forgotten herself as to allow them such licence and at last putting her behaviour down to the general oddness of the whole day.

"It's all very peculiar," she said to herself that night as she lay in bed. The windows were open to catch any breath of wind that might stir the warm air and she lay staring out at the dark night, unable to sleep, her mind a jumble of the days' events. "First the Prince noticing me and then the hussar . . . " She dwelt on the handsome soldier, remembering the bright, showy uniform he had worn, recalling above all the ruthless set to his mouth and, despite the heat of the night, a chill shiver ran down her spine. "I find that I don't care for you at all,

Captain Von Holstein," she said aloud. "It's a good thing that we will not meet again."

However, not many hours were to elapse before she discovered how wrong she was in her supposition; she and the children had finished their nursery supper to the faint sound of dance music from below and their nurse was just about to bear them away for their bath when a summons came for Miss Winter to present the two girls in the ballroom as soon as possible. Aghast, she and Nanny stared at each other while Rose and Daisy capered in glee.

"At this hour!" Rowan murmured incredulously.

"Best do what her ladyship wants," commented Nanny grimly, "and hope she doesn't keep the two mites downstairs too long. Come along, my ducks, let me put you into your best dresses like good girls."

With Rowan's aid the children were soon dressed in white muslin, one with a pink sash tied in an enormous bow behind her diminutive form, the other with a blue one.

"No time to curl their hair," sighed Nanny, wielding a brush vigorously.

"They look very pretty as they are," said Rowan, tying a bow on top of each of their shining heads to match the sashes.

"There, my poppets, you'll do," said their nurse, standing back to admire her work. "Be good and remember you're little ladies."

She could not resist sending the governess an admonishing glance as she spoke and Rowan knew she was thinking of the previous afternoon's escapade. With a heightened colour, she hurried her charges out of the nursery and down the stairs.

Gay music gradually grew louder as they drew near the ballroom and the little girls' grasps on her hands tightened with excitement, as the footman opened the double doors and they stood on the threshold, gazing entranced at the brilliant scene before them.

Ladies in beautiful gowns, jewels sparkling like raindrops, dipped and swayed in the arms of their partners, the black evening suits of the men making a sober contrast to their exuberant garb, while the occasional bright uniform gave its wearer the appearance of a peacock among his more humble brethren.

"Ooh," sighed Rose, ecstatically, hugging herself with delight. "If I were a grown-up lady, I'd dance and dance all night."

"There's Mama," Daisy pointed out, "and that soldier is with her."

Following the child's pointing finger, Rowan saw with a stab of something like dismay that she was right and Captain Von Holstein was standing beside his hostess. Meeting her eyes across the crowded room he allowed a small smile to show for a moment and almost imperceptibly bowed his head.

"She's beckoning — Mama wants us. We'd better go," said Rose urgently, tugging at her governess's hand, and Rowan withdrew her eyes with an effort from the bright grey ones and, recovering her composure, led the girls round the edge of the dance floor to their mother.

"There, Captain Von Holstein, you behold my chicks," she announced, dropping a kiss on each upturned face as she did so.

"As beautiful as their mother," the tall man responded gallantly. "In a few years you three will reign together, as society beauties. How envious of your enchanting looks and charm the other families must be."

Lady Devonish tapped his arm with her fan. "Flatterer," she laughed, obviously pleased with the fulsome compliments.

"Make your curtsys, girls, to the captain, for he asked leave for you to come down tonight as a special treat for you."

At her words Rowan looked up quickly and met the German's eyes above the two dancing bows that separated them and read an amused triumph in the grey gaze.

"Let me take them into the conservatory and ply them with refreshment, Lady Devonish," he said and, extricating himself with masterly aplomb, took a small hand in each of his and led the way to tall windows that opened on to an opulent jungle of hothouse plants.

Following reluctantly, Rowan found her charges seated together in the far corner of the conservatory behind a strategically placed and luxuriant shrub. "Isn't he *lovely?*" cried Rose, at her approach. "He's getting us some lemonade — and ice cream."

"It's too late for such things," Rowan began, but seeing their crestfallen expressions, relented. "Well . . . eat them slowly and don't get too excited." The blue-and-white figure quickly returned, bringing a footman bearing a tray.

"I thought you'd care for more adult delights," he observed, handing Rowan a tapering glass of sparkling liquid. "I hope you like champagne, Miss Winter." Lifting his own glass he smiled above the children's bent heads. "A toast," he said, "to a successful future."

"I should not — Lady Devonish — "

"Will never know," the hussar finished for her. "In my cousin's establishment you could drink champagne every day." His smile widened as she set the glass down with resolution. "Are you avoiding my toast, Fräulein?" he asked, his teeth gleaming in the dim light from the lanterns hanging among the shrubs and plants, "After all, what could be more

23

innocuous than a good future — for anyone?"

Rowan obeyed a sudden urge to be unconventional, for once to forget she was a governess and must bide by hidebound conventions and manners. Picking up the tall glass again she raised it in salute, "To the future," she said, "Which in my case I am sure will be very happy here at Hillington House."

Von Holstein's face altered almost imperceptibly, his mouth tightening and then relaxing as he bowed over his glass, "The future, Fräulein — whatever it may hold," he said lightly and then she was gathering up the girls and, despite their pleas, bearing them back to their nursery.

Their journey out of the ballroom took longer than she expected, so many were the kisses bestowed as each guest seemed to try to outdo the others in showing their love for children and delight in the girls' beauty. Rose accepted the accolade with cool pleasure, but Daisy soon grew tired of the strange faces bent to hers and hid her burning resentful face in her governess's skirts.

Just as they reached the door and in

a moment would have escaped, there was an outcry behind them as one of the guests made it dramatically known that her diamond necklace was no longer around her neck. With great presence of mind, the footmen closed the doors and stood impassively barring the way to any who would have left.

At Carl Von Holstein's suggestion, each guest examined the particular piece of floor upon which he happened to be standing, while servants searched the dining-room and conservatory. Murmurs of consternation and growing excitement filled the room when the diamonds were not found as each guest expressed their own particular theory of their whereabouts, while their owner, growing steadily more hysterical, had to be led away by her maid.

"There is nothing for it — we must all agree to be searched," said Captain Von Holstein, who seemed to have taken control.

"Oh, no," exclaimed Lady Devonish, while the guests gave shocked murmurs and drew instinctively away from their fellows, "I cannot have such a thing — "

"It's either that — or the police."

Lady Devonish gave a faint moan and shuddered. "Do what you will," she said and tottered to a nearby chair, laying back with her eyes closed and a vinaigrette held to her nose.

"Well, what is it to be?" inquired the hussar looking round. "Do we call in the police — or arrange matters among ourselves?"

Rowan moved and his eyes fell on her. Silently he raised his eyebrows.

"The children," she began, "they should not be here. May I take them away?"

For a moment he studied her, "I think not," he said at last. "At least not until we have decided what to do." Turning to his fellow guests he repeated his question and, at last, they reluctantly agreed to allow him to direct things.

"If three ladies and gentlemen will volunteer, they must first search each other and then all the guests in turn," Captain Von Holstein said, giving at least one of his listeners the impression that he had been involved in a similar happening before.

26

It was arranged as he suggested and soon the guests were obediently waiting their turn; the ladies in the dining-room and the men in the less salubrious surroundings of the conservatory. At last the three eminent ladies chosen for the unpleasant task announced themselves ready and the waiting women eyed one another uneasily, reluctant to be the first.

"Miss Winter, you were eager to take your charges away," said Captain Von Holstein maliciously, "Let Rose and Daisy go with their nurse and then you can follow."

Together they made their way to the hall, conscious that all eyes were upon them. Nanny received the girls into her capable hands and, almost without them realising it, it was quickly ascertained that the missing jewellery was not on them and they were led away to bed, scarcely aware of the unfortunate happenings in the ballroom.

"Now, Miss Winter," said one of the neat, black-clad maids, and Rowan stepped reluctantly forward and offered her reticule for inspection. Silently the women watched as the contents were tipped out on to a table hastily denuded of its linen covering and at once the watchers were struck into silence, while Rowan was unable to suppress a gasp of astonishment and dismay; amid a crumpled handkerchief and entangled with a few hairpins, a string of diamonds shone and sparkled with a cold beauty.

With a hand to her throat, Rowan stepped back, trying to deny all knowledge of the necklace with a voice grown hoarse and unmanageable. At a nod from one of the eminent women, a maid slipped across to stand in front of the door.

The elderly lady lifted her lorgnette and stared at Rowan coldly, "Go and tell them," she commanded, "to look no farther. We have found the thief."

# 2

"LADY DEVONISH will not see you, my dear," said the housekeeper to Rowan the next morning. "It is useless asking for an interview and, in my opinion, it is foolish to persist in this tale of yours that Captain Von Holstein put the necklace in your bag. Why, he is most respected. A member of the German aristocracy and here to put forward his cousin as a suitable wife for our own dear Prince; the Prince of Wales's eldest son."

Rowan clasped her hands in her lap, "Mrs Hollis, do you believe I didn't take it?" she asked quietly, her voice trembling for all her efforts to appear calm.

"Since you have been here I have formed a very high opinion of you, my dear." The housekeeper's voice was sympathetic, but she spread her hands in an hopeless gesture. "Under the circumstances, I can see nothing to be done."

"Must I leave quietly — with my future ruined, through no fault of my own? Because I am a nonentity no one believes me."

"I think that whoever was found to possess it would not have been believed. They were grateful to have found a scapegoat, and you, my dear, were unlucky. I can only advise you to go quietly, to fight them will only make matters worse, believe me."

"What shall I do?" Rowan asked dully.

"I can give you an address of an agency my sister runs in London, I shall explain the circumstances and my own faith in you and hope that she can find you a situation." Mrs Hollis wrote briskly and handed the note to Rowan.

"With no reference it will not be likely," Rowan made no attempt to hide the bitterness she felt as she accepted the scrap of paper.

"Have hope, my dear," advised the housekeeper and watched sadly as Rowan thanked her and left the room.

A short while later, she followed her tin box down the back stairs and watched as it was roped on the back of an ancient carriage by a footman. Glancing up, she saw the nursery curtains twitch and knew that Nanny had brought the children to watch her leave. She had not been allowed to say 'goodbye' to her charges and now she stepped forward and deliberately raised her hand in farewell. Two little hands appeared, waving briefly before they vanished and the net curtain was flicked back in place.

Sighing for the story Rose and Daisy had been told, Rowan climbed into the waiting vehicle and was driven away to the railway station. A train was drawing in as they approached. Rowan and her luggage were put on board and almost before she was settled in her seat, a whistle shrilled and they were on the way to London, amid clouds of steam and excited puffing from the engine.

Only having been to London once before and that as she passed through on her way to take up her position at Hillington House, she found the noise and bustle of the capital city rather overwhelming as she stepped out of Charing Cross station. A kindly cabby took her under his guidance and with his advice she soon found herself settled into a small boarding-house, whose genteel inmates seemed mainly to be governesses like herself either about to take up a new post, or in the throes of looking for a new position.

They greeted Rowan like a member of a sisterhood and, emboldened by their kindness, when she saw a picture of the Royal Family in a newspaper one woman was reading and caught sight of the name Von Holstein printed underneath she felt able to ask if she might borrow it for a few minutes.

"I, too, am very fond of our dear Royal Family," said the woman, having noticed what had taken Rowan's interest. "I take a great interest in their doings."

"Yes . . . a very admirable set of people," she answered absently, scanning the drawing for a likeness of the man she had met with such disastrous consequences, but concluding that beyond depicting a hussar's uniform, the artist had made no effort to draw more than a vague semblance of the typical German officer.

"You say you are interested in the Royal Family?" she asked suddenly, going on as the woman nodded. "Then perhaps you can help me. I met a Captain Von Holstein the other day, who offered me a position as governess with his cousin's family. Naturally, I would like to know more about the Count before I accept. Can you tell me anything about the Holsteins — I believe the captain is here to put forward one of the family as a suitable bride for the Duke of Clarence."

The other woman pursed her lips and stared thoughtfully at the window opposite, but it was clear that the passing traffic held no interest for her.

"Von Holstein . . . Von Holstein," she murmured. "Of course there are the Schleswig-Holstein-Sonderburg-Glucksburgs, who are the Royal Family of Denmark and our dear Princess of Wales's parents — but the Von Holsteins are a German branch. I rather think the Count's seat is on the Rhine. Drachenschloss, I believe it's called." She opened her eyes and smiled faintly at Rowan. "I have a dear friend who works in the College of Heralds. If you wished, I could ask her for information about them and let you know later."

Rowan thanked her and, after a few minutes, excused herself and went to her room even more puzzled by Captain Von Holstein's behaviour; the hussar gave no appearance of having fallen madly in love with her, well-educated governesses were easily available, she knew her antecedents well enough to know that she was no long-lost heiress to fabulous wealth or position. As far as she could see, the captain's odd behaviour could not be accounted for, and with a little gesture of irritated frustration, she jumped up from the bed on which she had been sitting and, jamming on her hat with scant regard for fashion, went in search of the agency run by Miss Hollis' sister.

An obliging policeman pointed her in the right direction and soon she was standing before a tall, narrow house, with a flight of stairs leading up to the front door. Inside, a group of women waited on hard chairs in the hall. Rowan found their general air of sombre gentility strangely depressing, knowing that in a few years she would give the same appearance; at the moment, she was still young enough and hopeful enough to allow herself a touch of individuality and wore a bunch of artificial flowers high on her shoulder with all the confidence of youth.

A short while later that confidence was somewhat dashed. Mrs Hollis's sister held out little hope for a position in the first front of families.

"Perhaps a shopkeeper . . . " she suggested shaking her head. "I feel the best we can hope for is a professional man's house. A doctor, a lawyer *might* take you — but with no reference from your last post . . . Tch, tch," and again she shook her head. "The bourgeoisie is more respectable than the aristocracy, you know," she said. "Come back in a few days and I will have found something for you."

Rowan felt that Mrs Hollis's sister was more kindly than truthful and left the agency despondently, so deep in thought about the predicament in which she found herself that she was quite unaware of the nondescript figure that followed her in the gathering dusk. Slipping from a concealing lamp-post, he kept a few paces behind her, matching his pace to hers but at no time did he seem about to intercept her. When she reached the boarding-house and hurried up the steps and in the front door, he strolled on casually, noting the house number with an almost imperceptible flick of his eyes and walking on without pausing.

A little after three the next afternoon, Rowan was surprised to receive a message that a gentleman wished to see her and was even more surprised to read the name on the card, the little housemaid held out to her.

Captain Von Holstein was waiting in the parlour and turned from his contemplation of an enormous copy of Landseer's 'Stag at Bay', which hung over the fireplace.

"My dear Miss Winter," he said, coming forward with a hand outstretched, "How kind of you to spare me your valuable time."

Unable to avoid his hand, Rowan allowed hers to lay in his grasp for the merest second, withdrawing it quickly.

"I was curious," she told him frankly.

"Come and take the air with me," he

suggested with a charming smile and conscious of the interest his presence invoked in the only other occupant of the room, who happened to be the inmate so preoccupied by royalty, Rowan assented against her better judgment and, a few minutes later, found herself on the German's arm, strolling along the hot summer street.

"How did you find me, Captain Von Holstein?" she asked.

"Mrs Hollis has a romantic heart . . . it took very little effort to persuade her to give me the address of her sister's agency. I only had to station a man in my employ outside, waiting until you called there, with instructions to follow you home and report back to me."

She could not but admire his enterprise. "And why did you go to such lengths to seek me out?"

Pausing in his stride, he half turned to her with a gesture indicating the lovely day. "The weather is so delightful it is a pity to waste it — and your charming company — in discourse. Grant me the pleasure, Fräulein, of giving you tea. I know a pleasant little establishment nearby where their cream cakes are nearly as good as those to be found in my country."

Rowan shook her head, disliking the word 'establishment' and aware of her emotions, the hussar's cold eyes gleamed momentarily with amusement.

"I do assure you that I am not recruiting for some potentate's harem," he said lightly, making his companion blush with the knowledge that he read her thoughts so easily. "Come then, to the Park, where we can listen to the band and take our refreshment in the open air — I could hardly abduct you under the eyes of so many people."

As she clearly wanted to know the reason behind his interest in her, Rowan agreed and found herself involuntarily admiring the ease with which he raised his cane and summoned a hansom cab.

In spite of the hot weather the Park was green and lush, filled with Londoners of all ranks enjoying the sun and freedom of an open space. Shopgirls and errand-boys dashed about on their employers' business, city gentlemen stole a few minutes from their offices, while nursemaids watched their charges and flirted sedately with passing soldiers, and members of society, eager to see and be seen, strolled elegantly along the gravel paths.

Carl Von Holstein seemed to have no difficulty in finding a table although most were taken and Rowan allowed him to order tea and cakes, while she slipped off her gloves and listened to the military band, that was playing the same selection that she had last heard at Lady Devonish's garden-party. Involuntarily, she glanced at her companion and, finding him watching her, knew by his expression that he was recalling the moment.

"I was sorry to learn of your troubles," he said quietly, making Rowan stifle an indignant gasp at his effrontery.

"To learn of it," she cried. "Why, you engineered it."

He frowned "I, Fräulein? What do you mean? Pray explain yourself."

Suddenly she found that one could not just say to the person opposite, "You took a valuable necklace and put it in my handbag," and avoiding his sharp grey gaze, lowered her own eyes and began to play with her teaspoon.

"You mean the search at Hillington House that found the diamonds in your reticule? My dear Fräulein, you must realise that if the police had been called in and found the same thing, you would not now be sitting here."

Rowan looked up, "I didn't take it," she said flatly. "Someone put it in my bag."

"Now, why would anyone do that?" he wondered, a note of derision in his voice that made Rowan lift her chin.

"I had supposed that someone wanted me dismissed from my position . . . but I imagine that the person who took it *might* have become frightened and, wishing to be rid of it, I was the nearest."

Von Holstein laughed, "I had not supposed you to possess such a dramatic imagination. Surely it's the lower classes who read those lurid paper books you call penny dreadfuls."

"Nevertheless, it was found on me and I was dismissed."

"Yes. Poor little Fräulein, how dreadful

for you." He leaned forward across the round top of the little iron table, "And that is why I have sought you out, Miss Winter. Now you have lost your post with Lady Devonish you will find it difficult to find another. Forgive me for mentioning a distressing subject, but Mrs Hollis told me in confidence that you were refused a reference. Therefore — I looked you up to renew my offer."

Rowan looked at him, "Ah, yes," she answered quietly. "How kind of you."

"Not at all," the captain said graciously. "Let me tell you a little of our family. The Holsteins are of very ancient lineage. The Princess of Wales is related to us — but remotely. She belongs to a cadet branch of the family. Drachenschloss was given to my ancestor by Frederick II in 1245 and we have lived there ever since, guarding the Rhine." He smiled proudly, the sunlight gleaming on his shining blond hair. "We take our age-old duties seriously, Miss Winter." Pausing for a few moments, he seemed occupied with his own thoughts. Before looking up, he assumed a brisk manner. "Doubtless you will want to know what the castle and surrounding countryside is like. Drachenschloss is a typical Rhineland castle, situated on a pinnacle of rock overlooking a fertile valley. While the castle is old, my cousin is wealthy enough to have had it modernised recently — we are proud of our water-closets and faucets. You'll find the local people friendly and completely loyal to the Von Holsteins."

"You make it sound very feudal."

"There is nothing wrong with loyalty, Fräulein. I myself owe loyalty to Count Otto. We are close kinsmen and grew up together and yet I count him my lord."

Rowan gazed at him thoughtfully. "And I am to look after the Count's children . . . How many are there?"

"Two. A boy and a girl."

She smiled and set down her cup. "How old are they and what are their names?" she asked.

"Seven and eight and they are called Gretchen and Hans."

"Hans is surely a little old to have a governess. Won't he be going away to school soon?"

"He has not been well. My cousin

thought it best for him to catch up with his school work first."

Rowan nibbled a biscuit, realising that in her position this was an opportunity not to be missed and yet some age-old instinct warned her against accepting the offer.

"Come, Miss Winter, we have sat here long enough. You must make up your mind, whether to accompany me or not when I leave for Germany."

"When will that be?"

"Thursday evening."

"But — that's only two days — "

"Long enough if you are a woman of decision, which I take you to be."

He watched her intently, his eyes holding hers, something in his pose telling her that her decision was important to him.

Swiftly she weighed the offer against her future as drawn by the woman who ran the governess agency and ignoring the warning sounding at the back of her brain, nodded agreement. "Very well," she said firmly. "I'll come."

"Good," he said curtly, though she had the impression that he was relieved. "I

43

will call for you after dinner on Thursday — we will drive down to Bradwell-on-Sea, where a yacht will be waiting." Taking out a slim leather wallet, he extracted a banknote and passed it to her discreetly. "Take it, Fräulein," he urged at her instinctive refusal. "Count it as part of your salary. There is much that you will need."

Rowan accepted the money reluctantly, knowing the truth of his words and yet unwilling to take charity from any but the closest of friends.

"There is the little matter of salary," she said delicately. "To manage my finances I would need to know — "

"Of course," Carl Von Holstein said smoothly. "What was Lady Devonish paying you?"

Rowan mentioned a sum and was astonished when the man opposite said calmly, "Double it."

"But — that is much too much," she gasped.

Gathering up his top hat and cane, Captain Von Holstein surveyed her. "You surprise me, Fräulein. If Count Otto, through me, offers you such a wage, then we think your services worth it. Accept it and be happy."

During the next days his advice was often in the forefront of Rowan's thoughts and she was happy as she spent more money on clothes than she had ever done before. Even when her father was alive, a clergyman's stipend did not allow extravagance in her wardrobe. For the first time in years, following Carl Von Holstein's suggestion, she did not feel forced to subdue her natural tastes and inclinations and limit her choice to dull colours and styles, feeling able instead to select with a clear conscience a velvet travelling suit, in the mauve shade made so fashionable by the Princess of Wales and also several pretty dresses and skirts.

The only discordant note was her own uncertainty that she was doing the right thing. This she resolutely put behind her, refusing to listen to the niggling doubts her mind presented. "Captain Von Holstein is so charming," she said to herself, "How could I have ever disliked him?" not admitting that under any other circumstances she would have wondered at his change of manner. Not only was she desperate for a situation, but suddenly her whole being craved excitement and adventure — which her proposed post in Germany seemed to offer, and ignoring the promptings of her common sense, she was determined for once in her life to leave security behind and take a chance upon the future.

The time to her appointment with the soldier seemed to fly and almost before she was ready the little maid-of-all-work told her that a gentleman had called for her. Straightening the waist of her new suit, Rowan pinned on the elegant mauve velvet pillbox hat, arranged the veil becomingly and went down stairs with a wildly beating heart.

Miss Wescott was obviously waiting for her at the foot of the stairs. The envelope she was holding out and her eager expression puzzled Rowan until she recalled the other's promise to find out about the Holsteins.

"How kind of you," she said, slipping the envelope into her handbag. "Do please thank your friend for going to so much trouble."

Miss Wescott hovered beside her as she crossed the hall. "Miss Winter, my dear Miss Winter," she murmured agitatedly, "I really do think you should read it — "

"But I will," Rowan assured her, "I am most interested in the Von Holsteins, but just now I am in rather a hurry. I've made up my mind to take the post, you see, and Captain Von Holstein is waiting in his carriage." She smiled and patted Miss Wescott's arm. "Thank you so much — I am most grateful, but I really must say goodbye. Perhaps we'll meet again some time."

Lifting her skirt, she ran down to the waiting carriage, leaving the other woman still advising the empty hall to 'read it first.'

"So — Miss Winter, you have not changed your mind?" said Carl Von Holstein, handing her into the luxurious interior.

"No. Why should I?" she asked, her eyes bright with excitement.

He shrugged, "No reason, but females are notorious for changing their decisions."

He smelt of brandy and cigars, and thinking of the meagre meal she had just consumed, Rowan was reminded of the very differing worlds they inhabited. Looking out of the window at the brightly lit theatres and houses and the busy, thronged streets she felt that she was gazing at the pages of a fashionable book. The satin upholstery was smooth and cool under her fingers and she settled back in her seat with a sigh of pleasure; all her life she had enjoyed journeys, and this promised to be the most exciting of her life. Even the thought of meeting with the unknown Count and his family could not detract from the delightful anticipation that filled her.

Captain Von Holstein seemed to have gone to sleep. He was leaning back against the cushions opposite her with his eyes closed and reminded of the note Miss Wescott had given her, Rowan gave way to curiosity and reached into her handbag for the envelope.

The flaring gas-lamps that lined the streets gave her plenty of light to see by and she found that she could read the thick, black writing easily.

"The Von Holsteins came to the fore during Frederick II's reign, when for their services to the crown they were given the title and Drachen Castle in the Rhineland and, leaving Holstein to a cadet branch of the family, they have resided there ever since, renowned for their bravery and ambition.

"Although much impoverished, they are known for their pride in their ancient lineage and recently a junior member of the family has been sent to England to put forward Countess Clara (the Count's sister — until the Count marries she carries the courtesy title) as a possible bride for the Duke of Clarence, which would improve the family fortune and further their ambitions.

"The heir to the estate and title at the moment is Captain Carl Von Holstein."

Looking up from the paper, Rowan found her companion's light gaze upon her.

"Not bad news, I hope?" he remarked.

"Rather — puzzling," she replied, folding the paper and slipping it back into her bag. "Forgive me — I have forgotten, but you did say the children were your cousin's, did you not?"

He nodded, watching her.

"And your cousin's wife — will she take an interest in their welfare?" Pleased with herself, she thought she had handled the matter delicately; after all, one could hardly ask if one was to teach the illegitimate offspring of a noble family.

"The Countess is rather a busy person — I dare say you will have a free hand with little Willie and Gretchen."

"*Hans*, surely, Captain Von Holstein."

"Hans Wilhelm to be exact," he answered easily, the red silk lining of his evening cloak catching fire from the street-lamps as they passed.

Suddenly Rowan made up her mind and, leaning forward, put her hand on the door latch. "Pray ask the driver to stop — I wish to be let down."

"May one ask why, Miss Winter?"

"You will think me the most foolish of females, but I find I cannot go through with this. The thought of the journey fills me with dread . . . Germany is so far away and I am afraid of the sea and being so far from home."

She saw that he was watching her intently, his face in shadows, the diamonds on his starched shirt front sparkling like stars in the dark interior. Suddenly his teeth gleamed in the darkness.

"You must indeed be foolish if you expect me to believe such nonsense, Fräulein, but whatever your reason it is too late now to go back on your word."

For answer, Rowan dragged at the door-handle and would have jumped from the moving vehicle, but for the fact that strong hands seized her, throwing her back against the padded cushions as the door was safely relocked.

"How dare you!" gasped Rowan, affronted at such treatment. "Set me down at once."

"To Germany you shall go, Fräulein, whether you wish it or not." Von Holstein answered curtly, stating a fact so certain that he was aware of no alternative.

"Indeed I will not," cried Rowan, enraged, springing to the other door, but before she could reach it, her hands were caught and she was thrust rudely back into the seat and for a moment lay still, her eyes wide.

"So now the game is over," said the man opposite reading the knowledge in her eyes and, hearing the satisfaction in his voice, Rowan wondered at the reason. "No more subterfuge," he went on and she suddenly realised how irksome it had been for him to set out to charm her into submission. "In the words of a melodrama, Miss Winter, you are in my power and will do as I say, or it will be the worse for you."

Reaching up to the driver's hatch above his head, he tapped on it with his gold topped cane. "Make all speed," he ordered when the hatch was lifted. "And stop for nothing." Seeing Rowan's face in the flaring gaslight, he smiled without amusement. "One of my men, Fräulein — and completely loyal to the Von Holsteins."

With her heart beating uncomfortably fast, Rowan lay back, studying the man opposite, almost unable to believe that such a thing could be happening to her and half inclined to think that she was in the throes of a particularly vivid nightmare. However, the pain in her fingers, caused by the way she was clasping the handle of her handbag, so tightly that the metal edge dug into her flesh, convinced her of the reality of the happening.

"You can't really be abducting me," she said uncertainly. "Such things do not happen nowadays."

Von Holstein's teeth gleamed again in a manner to which she was fast taking a dislike, making her marvel silently that she could ever have been so foolish as to allow herself to be taken in by his charming manner.

"You have just found that they do," he answered. "Be good — be reasonable and do as you are told and, when it is all over, you will find yourself well paid."

"And if I don't?" Rowan was forced to ask.

His mouth straightened slowly and even in the uncertain light she could see how uncompromisingly ruthless was his expression. "Do not contemplate such an action, Fräulein," he warned, and Rowan felt herself grow cold at the grim note in his voice.

# 3

GRADUALLY the busy thorough-fares of the City were left behind and meaner, less well-lit streets took their place until even these gave way to fields and cottages as the carriage took the Colchester road out of London. For a while they drove on in silence, Rowan too busy planning various means of escape and Von Holstein too satisfied to feel the need for conversation.

"Do you really believe you can get away with this?" Rowan demanded at last, having considered and discarded many plans and schemes.

Carl Von Holstein raised his eyebrows, "If I did not believe so I would not have attempted it," he told her. "No one will come looking for you, Fräulein, you are too insignificant."

"And you, Captain, are ill-mannered!" Rowan glowered at him, too angry to remember her lowly position.

He shook his head, "No — merely

truthful. You, Miss Winter, have no near relatives to wonder where you are and no influential friends to seek you out. You are a nothing — a nobody. Miss Rowan Winter will vanish from sight and no one will even notice."

Rowan swallowed convulsively, realising the truth of his words while for the first time fear settled heavily in the pit of her stomach. Her eyes grew wide and dark in her white face as she stared across the dim interior.

"Do not be afraid," the German told her, his tone less harsh. "If you do as you are told, not only will no harm come to you, but you will be well paid."

"Why are you doing this — what do you want with me?"

"Have patience, Fräulein, you will know in good time. Be content with the knowledge that we are driving along the Colchester road and will shortly turn off towards the charming little village of Bradwell-on-Sea, where a yacht is awaiting us. Relax, sleep if you will, but be quite sure there is nothing you can do to circumvent my plans."

"I'll tell you, plainly, Captain Von

Holstein that I have no intention of meekly obeying you. I will not — "

"You bore me, Miss Winter. Of *course* you will do as I wish. If I considered you at all, I supposed you a woman of intelligence, but to even consider disobeying me is extremely foolish . . . as well as dangerous."

Rowan lifted her chin and her mauve velvet bodice rose and fell with the agitation of her breathing, but, biting her lip, she refrained from making any comment. Turning her shoulder on her companion she gazed ostentatiously out of the window at the dark countryside flashing by. Some time later, the carriage slowed its headlong speed, turned off the well-made road and proceeded more cautiously along a narrow, winding lane that turned and twisted past flat fields and tiny villages of neat, clapboard houses.

The uncomfortable, jolting journey continued for some while. Then they drove through a small village, its windows heavily curtained, and about a mile farther on they came to a stop on a stone quay above a small sand and shingle beach. As Von Holstein rolled down the window the smell of the sea filled Rowan's nostrils and the dull pounding of the waves on the beach told her that they had reached their intermediate destination.

After exchanging a few quick words in German with the man outside the captain drew in his head and turned to Rowan as he collected his top hat and cane.

"We have arrived," he announced. "The yacht is at the end of the quay. It is late at night and the only people about are my men, so feel free to scream or beg for help if it will relieve you — I assure you it will avail nothing else."

He climbed down from the carriage and turned to give his hand to Rowan. Pausing in the doorway, she studied her surroundings and saw that her companion had spoken the truth; apart from the driver and groom, there were only two sailors on the quay and they wore the flat caps with long ribbons that proclaimed their nationality. The moon had risen and showed clearly the yacht tied up nearby, her empty masts silhouetted against the dark night sky.

"Come along, Miss Winter," said Carl

Von Holstein impatiently, his hand held out. "We will sail when the tide turns and it will be more comfortable for you if you are settled in your cabin before then."

Rowan allowed herself to be helped down the steps, but removed her fingers from his grasp as soon as her feet were firmly on the stone causeway. A rough wind from the sea snatched at her hat and wrapped the wide folds of her skirt about her legs and, to her chagrin, she had to accept the aid of his arm to make her way against the buffeting gale. By the time they reached the yacht she was breathless and felt as if she had been tugged and pushed by a hundred unfriendly hands and at first, when she entered the warmth and comfort of the luxurious boat she was only aware of relief that the unpleasant sensations were over. Looking about, as she gradually recovered her equilibrium, she took in the dark, shining woodwork, brightly polished brass and the all pervading smell of oil that hung heavily in the air.

"I do hope you are not troubled by *mal de mer*," said the soldier politely, not without a certain grim amusement as he read her growing unease as the engines sprang to throbbing life under their feet.

"This is Helga," he said as a tall, severe-faced woman in a black dress approached silently. "She will 'maid' you during the journey to Drachenschloss."

The woman inclined her head and her eyes swept over Rowan without a flicker of a smile. Picking up the overnight case which the captain had brought from the carriage she turned and glided away, her long skirt rustling over the wooden deck.

"Go with Helga, Miss Winter — you will find her very capable, if not communicative."

Seeing no other course of action, she obeyed him reluctantly and followed the tall figure of the maid through a narrow wooden door and found herself in a small, but luxuriously appointed cabin. Helga was already unpacking and dextrously slipping underwear and toiletries away in the many drawers that formed a dressing-table against one wall.

"I suppose you know I am here against my will," Rowan said in German, unpinning her hat and dropping it on the bunk that filled the far side of the cabin.

"If you say so, Fräulein," said Helga, without looking up from her task and with no show of interest.

"Captain Von Holstein is abducting me."

"The captain never does anything without a good reason, miss."

"And that makes the fact that I've been kidnapped perfectly all right?"

"It's none of my business, miss. I'm here to look after you — nothing more."

"So you won't help me to escape?"

"No." A grim smile crossed her thin mouth. "I believe we have just sailed, miss, so it would be a little late."

With dismay Rowan became aware that the dull thudding of the engines which had filled her ears since coming on board had changed and became more urgent, while the deck underfoot vibrated like a live thing, convincing her of the truth of the other woman's words. Reaching above the rows of drawers, she pulled back the curtains that covered the porthole and peered through the tiny, round opening, only to see an exposure of velvet blackness, with a few twinkling lights that were rapidly passing out of view.

For a moment she poised on tiptoe, contemplating making a dash for the deck in the hopes of being able to throw herself back on to the quay, but one look at Helga's wary stance and indomitable size, made her realise that the maid was not only aware of her thoughts but that she could easily overpower her if it came to a struggle. The realisation of the indignity she would suffer made Rowan put aside all thoughts of a physical contest between herself and the other and she forced herself to relax, perceptibly, while she became increasingly aware of a feeling of growing queasiness as the deck dipped and swayed under her feet.

Sitting down abruptly, she put a hand to her mouth and closed her eyes, suddenly unable to bear the sight of the swaying curtains.

"If you'll take my advice, Fräulein, bed is the best place," came Helga's sensible voice, and competent hands took hold of her.

Unable to resist, should she have

wanted to, Rowan felt herself undressed and put to bed like a baby. Relieved to put her spinning head on the cool pillow, she lay still, hoping the unpleasant sensations would soon pass, but inevitably she was forced to accept the maid's ministrations and passed the night in acute misery as the yacht headed out into the Channel. By the early hours, however, she fought her way into deeper, calmer waters and was sailing towards the Dutch coast. As the first flash of dawn streaked the sky, Rowan fell into an exhausted sleep and awoke some hours later to clear skies and bright sunshine.

For a while she gazed at the sight of the curtains' gentle movement, afraid to move in case she brought back a return of the *mal de mer*, but at last she summoned up enough courage to sit up and cautiously swing her legs over the side of the bunk. Nothing untoward happened and, much encouraged, she stood up and proceeded to wash and dress quickly. Never having been on board a boat before she found herself somewhat nonplussed concerning what to wear, but recalling pictures she had seen of the Royal Family sailing off Cowes, on the Isle of Wight, she chose a white serge skirt and plain blouse as most suitable. Thus attired she left her cabin, secretly relieved to find the door was not locked, and climbed the companionway to the open deck.

As she stepped on to the deck she was greeted by a breeze that lifted her hair and cooled her hot cheeks. Two sailors looked up at her arrival and one hurried away while the other watched her warily. Nodding coolly, she went to the rail and, leaning her arms on it, lifted her face into the wind, enjoying the freedom after the hours confined to her cabin.

"Good morning, Fräulein. I trust you are feeling better? Helga informed that you were indisposed during the night."

Turning, she saw that Carl Von Holstein had come on deck, warned no doubt, of her appearance by the first sailor. Tight, white linen trousers and a shirt open at the neck highlighted his slim figure and broad shoulders, while the sun shone on his fair hair, giving him the appearance of owning a halo.

Without waiting for an answer he

went on. "Come and have breakfast. No need to look down your nose — I do assure it is much the best thing and will restore you."

Taking her arm, he led her to a table and chairs under a striped awning, sheltered from the breeze by the superstructure. Holding a chair for her, he waited until she was seated before taking the chair opposite and shaking out his crisp, white napkin. Reluctantly, Rowan accepted toast and marmalade, eating at first hesitantly, but soon discovering that she was unexpectedly hungry, finished the meal with evident enjoyment.

Wiping the crumbs from her mouth with the napkin, she glanced up to meet the German's amused gaze.

"I think the time has come for an explanation, Herr Von Holstein," she said with some asperity.

He raised his eyebrows, and finished lighting a cigar before replying. "Do you, indeed," he said thoughtfully, watching a smoke ring being dispersed by the sea breeze.

"Yes," Rowan answered boldly. "To have gone to such lengths you must have some good reason. I am too well aware of my lack of looks to believe that you have abducted me with amorous intentions."

She stopped, aware that his mobile brows had risen again, and flushed a little, somewhat disconcerted by the frankness of his gaze as his eyes travelled over her face and form.

"Now there you underestimate yourself, Fräulein," he said. "True, you are not conventionally pretty, which implies a fashionable insipidness, but with the right clothes and hairstyle you will find you have something more."

Rowan's eyes had widened at his words and while the first fright she had felt had abated slightly overnight, now she felt her fears returning. In his informal clothes, with his tanned skin and proud, arrogant air, the man before her had the appearance of every villain ever portrayed on the stage or in a book.

After a final draw on his cigar, Carl Von Holstein threw the butt overboard and, reaching into his pocket, drew out a small object and placed it on the table before Rowan. "Open it," he commanded.

Reluctantly she picked up the oval

gold locket and, with fingers that shook slightly, fumbled for the catch. Suddenly it sprang open and she found herself gazing at a girl of about her own age, with the dark masses of her hair swept in a fashionable style, her vivid face tilted a trifle as she surveyed the world with an undeniably challenging air.

"Do you recognise her?"

Rowan lifted her eyes, a puzzled frown between her brows. "She seems familiar . . . and yet — "

"You see someone remarkably like her every morning in the mirror."

For a moment she stared at him, blankly, her own gaze wide and bewildered, before returning her eyes to the painted face smiling up at her.

"Oh, yes, with the right hairstyle and gown the likeness will be astonishing. Even your Prince of Wales noticed it."

Rowan's heart jolted as she recalled the Prince's words at the garden party that had so puzzled her.

"But who — why — ?" she made a helpless little gesture, unable to put her bewilderment into words.

"The lady is my cousin, the Countess

Clara. As to why, that is a much longer tale. Doubtless you are aware that your own Royal Family is looking out for a suitable bride for the heir to the throne. The Von Holsteins have put forward our own delightful candidate, but, unfortunately, Clara is indisposed, with an illness which is likely to be of some months' duration. Now, even you, Miss Winter, must know that no royal bride may have any but the most robust of health. It seems hardly fair that Clara, who normally enjoys more than her share of vigour and vitality, should lose her chance to be queen merely due to the inconsiderate nature of some microbe. What do you think?"

"Well . . . it does seem a little unfortunate."

"Exactly. And even more so as Queen Victoria has ordered her eldest daughter, who is also our Empress, to inspect the prospective brides, with an eye to their suitability."

"But why kidnap me — how can I help?"

He smiled a little. "I think you already know, Miss Winter," he said slowly.

"You must be mad!"

"Oh, no. It seems a very good idea to me."

"For me to take the Countess's place? It's quite impossible."

"A little difficult, perhaps, but nothing is impossible, Fräulein, to someone with determination."

Rowan shook her head. "I won't do it," she stated positively. "You can't make me."

"I said nothing was impossible to a person of determination, if you remember. Well, I, Fräulein, have a nature of the utmost determination." He leaned closer across the table, holding her eyes with his. "Let me assure you that life will become very unpleasant for you if you don't do as I wish . . . " For a moment he let the menace in his voice sink in and then went on, "Whereas, if you please me, you will return home, nothing the worse and considerably more wealthy."

Rowan's common sense told her to appear to concede to his wishes; at the moment she was totally in his power. Later, when they had landed, circumstances would be different and she might find the opportunity to escape from what appeared to be a dangerous situation.

"People will notice . . . There might be a superficial likeness but, to anyone who knows the Countess, the substitution would be obvious," she objected, making her voice sound hesitant as though she was wavering upon the verge of allowing herself to be persuaded.

"Such things can be managed, believe me. You would stay in Drachenschloss, in seclusion, as we do every summer. Only trusted servants would see you closely. Friends and acquaintances could be avoided. It need only be known that the Countess Clara is seen to be well — that no rumours start up about her."

"I will think it over," she told him and, to her relief, he sat back, obviously satisfied.

"I thought you would," he observed indifferently and, having got his way, made no effort to hide the fact that he had lost all interest in Rowan. "We will dock some time tonight and take the train in the morning. Feel free to do as you wish until then."

And without bothering to make an excuse, he rose and walked away. Watching his retreating figure, Rowan felt perversely chagrined by his treatment; while she did not exactly care for his high-handed ways, she had no liking to be subjected to complete indifference and found it hardly flattering when he made it so obvious that his only interest in her had been with his impossible scheme in mind. Somewhat to her surprise, for she had thought she had suppressed it long ago, she found that even a lowly governess had her pride and eyed his blond head with dislike.

"Just wait, Captain Carl Von Holstein," she promised under her breath. "You'll find I'm not so meek and mild as you suppose."

True to his word, they dropped anchor in the early hours of the next morning, and Rowan, who had been awaiting such an event, slipped her legs over the side of her bunk and peered cautiously out of the porthole. The moon was still high and in its clear radiance she could see a flat shoreline nearby and a huddle of buildings lining the water's edge. The yacht appeared to have halted some yards away from the quayside, not as she had hoped within jumping distance of land. However, during the long waiting hours she had made a plan for just such a contingency as this and, slipping out of her top clothes, she bundled her jacket and skirt together, tying them with a scarf and, having concealed her state of undress beneath a dark cloak, she opened her cabin door and made her way silently to the deck.

To her relief no one was about, the holystoned deck-planks gleamed white in the moonlight and were totally deserted. Cautiously, she crossed to the side nearest the shore, dropped her cloak and climbing over the iron rails, let herself quietly down into the black water with scarcely a betraying splash. Holding her bundle above her head, she began to swim one-handed towards the beach and, as she did so, an excited shout from the yacht told her that she had been seen. She glanced behind in time to see a figure jump from the railings and enter the water in a long, low dive. Discarding her skirt and jacket she put on speed in an effort to escape, recognising with dismay that the man behind was an expert swimmer and, good as she was, she stood very little chance of outdistancing him.

Controlling her breathing with an effort, she plunged on, concentrating on shortening the distance to the dark silhouettes of the houses that lined the harbour. Without warning, a hand grasped her ankle, dragging her down below the surface of the sea. Holding her breath, she turned on her captor, kicking and scratching in an effort to be free. The grip on her ankle loosened and for a moment she thought she had won, as she shot to the surface and opened her mouth for a gasp of air. Hands seized her shoulders and she was plunged under again, filling her mouth with salt water. The man leaned on her, holding her down by his weight and strength until Rowan felt her own strength leave her as sea water burned her throat and she turned weak and dizzy from lack of oxygen.

Suddenly her head was above the surface again and while she drew great breaths of air into her panting lungs, hands seized her and she was dragged over the gunwale of a small boat. For a while she lay in the bottom, gasping and shivering, dimly aware of the sound of rowlocks creaking and grunts of effort from above her. Gradually her head cleared and she realised that she was being rowed back to the yacht she had just left. Her sudden, convulsive movement made the man seated above her look down and with a stare she recognised, in the wet, half-clothed figure, the usually immaculate hussar.

"You!" she gasped, staring up, her voice hoarse from the sea water she had swallowed.

Von Holstein shook back the dripping hair that clung to his skull and put a restraining hand on her shoulder. "I had no idea that you had a liking for aquatic sports, Miss Winter," he responded. "I own that you surprise me."

Rowan shivered and sniffed, wiping her wet face and hair with her hands, but was saved from making a suitable reply by the boat thudding gently against the side of the yacht. A rope ladder was thrown to them and, apparently feeling her incapable of mounting by such a means, Von Holstein flung her over one shoulder and, despite her vociferous protests, carried her to the deck above.

Setting her none too gently on her feet, he retained his grip on her arm, holding her away from him while he let his gaze wander over her.

Acutely aware of her soaking drawers and chemise clinging to every curve of her wet body, Rowan flushed but, instead of lowering her eyes, lifted her chin and stared defiantly up at him.

"A gentleman, Herr Von Holstein, would offer me a covering," she said angrily.

He smiled briefly, his teeth gleaming momentarily in the waving moonlight. "A lady, Miss Winter, would never have got herself into such a predicament. However . . . " For a moment longer he held her gaze, before releasing her with a gesture to someone behind her.

A welcoming warmth enveloped her shivering body as a cloak was wrapped round her shoulders.

"Go with Helga," he went on. "There is just time for a bath before we land." Seeing her astonished face he smiled again. "Did you think your attempt to escape would make any difference? How foolish you are, Fräulein . . . it merely adds a certain enjoyment to the game, which I must confess I had thought a trifle dull."

After flicking her chin with one finger in a careless gesture he walked away, leaving her staring after his retreating figure; his gaze had certainly held more than indifference during the last few minutes and Rowan was not at all sure she cared for the change. His gleaming pale eyes had distinctly reminded her of a cat enjoying the pleasures of the hunt and the thought of herself as his helpless, mouselike prey, she found extremely unnerving.

"Come, miss," Helga urged her towards the companionway. "I have a bath waiting."

Rowan looked at her, "You were so sure he would bring me back?"

"Oh, yes. I never doubted it. The captain always does what he sets out to do."

The bath was hot and perfumed, but Rowan was not allowed to linger in its scented depths. Helga towelled her hair ruthlessly and by the time she was dressed in her white frilly petticoat it was dry enough for the maid to arrange it in a fashionable style. Rowan expected to wear her mauve travelling ensemble, but was surprised to see Helga take an elaborate royal blue velvet skirt and bodice from the wardrobe.

"That's not mine," she said quickly.

"It's what the captain wishes you to wear." For a moment the older woman held her eyes, reading the intentions to rebel, before she added flatly. "You'll have to, miss, unless you've a liking to land in your petticoats, for I've packed the rest and they've been taken ashore."

Realising her defeat, Rowan accepted the gown with as good a grace as she could muster, even admitting to herself, as she examined her reflection in the mirror, that the tight bodice with its row of tiny gold buttons and the slim, bell-shaped skirt, with a hint of a bustle, was more becoming than anything she had ever owned.

"You're the image of the Countess," said Helga from behind, and their eyes

76

met in the mirror. "Oh, I know what he's planning — you're as like as two peas."

Rowan watched her thoughtfully and, as though reading her mind, the other went on speaking while she deftly pinned a little feather toque in place and arranged the veil.

"There's not much I don't know concerning the Holsteins. I've been with the family since I was a child and my parents and grandparents before me and right back as long as there've been Holsteins, I dare say. They are a family to be proud of — they're a law unto themselves and only admit allegiance to the Kaiser. The very name shows they're different. Others use a small v for the von, but not they — they've always used a capital letter."

"Why?" Rowan could not restrain from asking.

Helga shrugged. "To be different, I expect." Having arranged the hat to her satisfaction, she stood back to survey her handiwork. "Well, I'd say you'd pass for the Countess Clara anywhere," she declared, and Rowan looked in the mirror to meet the eyes of the double of the girl in the locket.

Carl Von Holstein's eyes widened momentarily as she appeared on deck. "Well done, Helga," he smiled to the maid at her shoulder. "You are to be congratulated."

Ignoring him, Rowan looked around and saw that during the time she had spent in her cabin they had moved and were now tied up alongside the harbour wall. A pile of luggage had already been unloaded on to the quay and was being stowed in a wagon.

"Time we went ashore, Fräulein," said the soldier and, taking her hand, tucked it into his elbow, holding it firmly against his side. "I beg you to give up all thoughts of escape. It would be . . . unsuccessful."

Rowan tossed him a scornful look and tilted her chin, realising with wry amusement that she seemed to have left her sanguine behaviour behind with her governess clothes. Her challenging expression seemed not to worry her captor, rather he met her glance with amusement and nipped her fingers painfully.

"Behave, Fräulein," he cautioned and led her down the gangplank.

# 4

IT was very early in the morning and the little town was only just waking. A few urchins looking for pennies were about, sailors were swabbing the decks of their ships and one or two diligent housewives were virtuously whitening their front steps; an office performed by sleepy maids for the more wealthy households. No one was wide enough awake to display any interest as the little procession passed and not until they reached the new railway station did Rowan see anyone who might be a possible ally.

Passing under the elaborate stone portal, she reflected silently that railway architecture was obviously much the same the world over. At the entrance to a draughty platform they were met by a large, beaming gentleman in a heavily braided uniform.

Twirling his magnificent moustaches, he made an elegant bow. "A hundred welcomes to my humble station, Your Excellencies," he rumbled in a voice to match his physique.

Feeling as if she had discovered Father Christmas in his summer disguise, Rowan stepped forward. "*Mein Herr*," she said in German, "I am being abducted. Pray send for the police to arrest these people."

His expression faltered and grew still, but with a valiant effort he kept the smile on his face, while above her head his eyes sought those of Von Holstein. After a barely perceptible pause, he took her outstretched hand and carried it to his lips, "My dear lady," he said, giving it a paternal pat, "may I say how charming you are looking? Let me lead you to your carriage — where everything is of the most luxurious, as your husband ordered."

"Didn't you hear me — I'm being held against my will — " Rowan broke off to stare at him. "*Husband*, did you say? I haven't got a husband!"

"So sad, so sad," he murmured and mopped his brow with a large white handkerchief, eyeing Carl Von Holstein with undisguised sympathy.

"Now, now, *liebling*, behave," said the hussar behind her and, before she could move, his arm encircled her waist while his other hand gripped her arm firmly. "Come along to the carriage like a good girl."

She was almost lifted off her feet and half carried along the platform to where a resplendent chocolate-brown train waited, quietly puffing steam into the still, morning air.

Helga hurried ahead and, having mounted the high step, turned in the doorway of the carriage to receive her. As she was bundled up through the door Rowan caught hold of the frame and, turning in the soldier's arms, made a last, desperate appeal to the uniformed figure hovering on the platform.

"Help me — *please* help me," she cried.

"Control yourself my dear," urged Von Holstein in her ear. "You are embarrassing the stationmaster."

The truth of his statement was patently clear; even the enormous moustache seemed to drop in acute discomfort, while the protuberant eyes watered slightly with sympathy.

"My condolences, dear sir," he murmured. "So young — so beautiful — " And once again he had recourse to the large handkerchief.

"If we could leave as soon as possible . . . " Carl Von Holstein suggested delicately.

"Of course — I quite understand," agreed the stationmaster and, eager to please, strode off briskly towards the engine, still shaking his head occasionally.

The soldier bustled Rowan along a narrow corridor and into what appeared to be a long drawing-room somewhat overfurnished, with plush armchairs, well-polished tables and draped curtains at the windows.

"Our private coach," he pointed out, releasing her. "No one will disturb us until we get to our destination."

Having taken in her surroundings with a quick glance, Rowan turned back to her captor to glare at him, her brows drawn together in a scowl.

"Now, why are you glowering at me like a little fighting cock," he queried, not hiding his amusement.

"What did you say to that — that imbecile?"

He shrugged. "That the weather promised to be nice — that the sea-trip was pleasant."

"You know what I mean," Rowan burst out impatiently. "Why wouldn't he listen to me?"

"I told him that you had the misfortune to be mad," the hussar told her pleasantly.

"Oh!" she gasped and sought in vain for words to express her indignation and rage. Before she could give voice to her seething emotions, there was a piercing whistle and the train started with a jolt that jerked her forward into the German's arms.

Finding herself clasped firmly to a broad masculine chest, Rowan was at first too surprised to move and then was galvanised into sudden action, but found to her dismay that her struggles were easily restrained.

"Let me go," she demanded.

"Has anyone told you, Miss Winter, that a rage becomes you?" her captor asked outrageously. "Your eyes are very fine when they are sparkling with temper and that high colour can only be described as attractive."

Rowan flung up her head to eye him stormily but, warned by some age-old instinct, grew still in his grip.

"You take advantage of your position — and mine," she said coldly and with a creditable attempt at calm, for all the buttons on her bodice rose and fell quickly with her hidden agitation.

"I am afraid it is a habit men have," she was told lazily and, slowly, he bent his head to kiss her.

Surprised by his action, Rowan felt the hot blood of sheer fury race through her veins. Rage at such treatment consumed her and, dragging one hand free, she struck him across the cheek with all her strength.

"How dare you!" she raged. "I loathe and despise you."

Catching her hand as she raised it again, Carl Von Holstein stared down at her. "Because I kissed you?" he asked. "You despise me because I kissed you?"

"Because you treated me like a — a light woman. You would not have treated your social equal so."

"Ah — I see. It is your pride which is hurt. Well, let me tell you, little miss, that my *social equal* would have given me my kiss most willingly. We are not bound by the staid morals of the lower classes."

Involuntarily recalling the gossip she had heard at Hillington House, Rowan was forced to admit to the truth of his statement.

"So — you see I have paid you two compliments. One, I have treated you as my equal and two, I have kissed you, which I have wanted to do for sometime."

"That is not true!" she exclaimed, so indignant at such a blatant lie that for a moment she forgot the original cause of her anger. "You felt the utmost indifference to me, save that I might be of use to your precious Clara, until this morning . . ."

Her voice trailed away and her eyes fell under the glance of bold amusement with which he was regarding her, while a burning spot appeared high on each cheekbone.

"Pre-cisely," he drawled. "Until you stood before me newly taken from the sea I had failed to realise the attraction mermaids held for the men who found them. Let us say, Miss Winter, that your attempt to escape made me look at you with totally new eyes."

"I don't believe it's the first time you've seen a woman in her underwear," Rowan told him, conscious of her own embarrassment and his amusement, "but I do believe that until then you had only thought of me as a — a pliable doll to be manipulated in your grand design. Now you are surprised to discover I am a person — though I don't think you realise I have feelings and emotions just like women of your class."

Carl Von Holstein's face changed and, releasing her, he stepped back. For a moment he continued to regard her, his eyes bleak in a taut face, before drawing himself up to his full height, he clicked his heels together and bowed stiffly.

"My apologies, Fräulein. In future I shall take care to remember that you are no automaton."

He sat himself in one of the plush

86

chairs and stared moodily out of the window, leaving Rowan relieved that she had cooled his ardour for the moment, but uneasily aware that the cold stranger might prove more dangerous.

After a while she seated herself on the other side of the carriage and watched the flat countryside speeding by. By the numbers of windmills dotted among the green fields and straight canals, she gathered that the train must be crossing Holland and, recalling the geography she taught to her pupils, fell to working out the whereabouts of their final destination. Holstein, she knew from learning about the events of forty years before when Germany annexed the principality, was situated in the north, bordering Denmark, but the castle of the Von Holstein's, she felt sure, was nearer the middle of the country.

About midday Helga appeared with two picnic baskets which she presented to the silent travellers. The Dutch scenery soon palled and Rowan found herself envying her companion the book in which he was engrossed. Apparently realising her boredom, Von Holstein, when next the train drew into a station, lowered a window and called over a newspaper vendor, purchasing a periodical, which he presented to her.

Finding herself the possessor of a copy of the *Strand Magazine*, Rowan settled down to pass the time in reading, but found difficulty in concentrating on the small print. Uneasily aware of the man opposite, she found herself stealing glances at his bent head, until happening to look up unexpectedly, he caught her eye and held her gaze with his. Somewhat disconcertingly he rose and came to stand beside her.

"I owe you an apology, Miss Winter," he said, "I see now that I should have taken you into my confidence at Lady Devonish's house. You are undoubtedly an intelligent woman and if I had put the matter before you clearly and made my offer, I feel sure that you would have felt able to help me without all this melodramatic subterfuge." His smile was charming and Rowan felt herself respond involuntarily. "So let us start this acquaintance again. Indulge me, Fräulein, and pretend you have never met this dolt of a hussar before. I have just been presented to you . . . "

Taking her hand, he clicked his heels and bowed formally. "May I sit beside you, Fräulein?" he went on as if they had just been introduced. "Forgive me if I stare — but you are the image of my cousin."

"I have heard that everyone has a double," said Rowan, entering into the game.

"Perhaps . . . But to see you, Miss Winter, is to believe that the Countess Clara is sitting beside me." His eyes travelled over her in frank admiration. "The same dark hair, the identical, delightful face, her own, wilful, rebellious mouth . . . "

Rowan flushed and looked away, but a hand cupped her chin and turned her to face him. "I think the angels must have sent you, Miss Winter, for the Von Holsteins have desperate need of you."

Reluctantly forced to meet his eyes, Rowan felt herself drowning in his gaze, totally unable to look away.

"Let me tell you a story, Fräulein. A long time ago there were three children, two were the children of the Count of Drachenschloss — the third was a poor cousin, whose impoverished parents had died in his infancy. That unfortunate boy was brought up in the castle, so kindly and with such love, that until he was adult he had no idea that he *was* unfortunate. I was the boy, Miss Winter, and I owe such a debt to my kinsmen that I fancy I shall die with my gratitude still unpaid."

Rowan looked at him, seeing the tow-headed child behind the proud, aquiline features of the man beside her.

"Now we must come to the present day. The Von Holsteins, once the richest family on the Rhine, have fallen on hard times; they need to replenish their coffers and see an opportunity to do this when they hear that the Dowager Empress is looking about for a suitable bride for her nephew, who will one day be the King of England and she discreetly makes it known that her eye has fallen upon the Countess Clara. Imagine the hope, the excitement! But all to no avail, poor Clara is ill — are all our hopes to be dashed because of such bad luck?

90

Clara's indisposition must take its course, but, in the meantime, the little bride will be chosen and Clara Von Holstein passed over. Think, then, Miss Winter, of the hope your appearance raised in my breast. I did not consider you — and for this I apologise — but thought only that I would be able to help my cousins in their need."

Carl Von Holstein spoke earnestly and Rowan felt herself warming to him as he made his confession.

"You should have told me — if I had known . . . " she murmured, allowing him to take her hand and raise it to his lips.

"I should have known that you were a woman of compassion," he said, "but I did not consider more than that here was a heaven-sent chance to repay my kinsmen for their kindness to me. A kind of madness seized me, I could think of nothing save that I must not be thwarted and I lost sight of the fact that you were a person in your own right . . . My upbringing is somewhat to blame. In their principality the Von Holsteins hold almost feudal state, their word is law — and some little of that attitude has adhered to me. Now — I throw myself upon your kind heart. If you wish, we will turn the train round at the next station and you can return to England, but if you could find it in your heart to help us, you will find the Von Holsteins . . . grateful."

Taking a deep breath, the girl smiled, "I've always wanted to travel," she said simply.

"You have earned the gratitude of the Holsteins," the hussar told her grandly, before glancing at his watch. "There is just time to dress before dinner," he said, "let me escort you to your room."

Rowan allowed him to lead her out of the carriage and into a corridor with a row of five doors leading off.

"The kitchen, the servants' rooms and our bedrooms," announced Von Holstein, opening the doors briefly to allow her a glimpse inside the various rooms.

"H-how grand," said Rowan faintly, overcome by the opulence.

"Oh, we have every comfort," said Von Holstein. "There is no other way to travel."

Marvelling a little, Rowan entered the room indicated and, closing the door behind her, leaned against it while taking in her surroundings. Apart from the fact that it was more narrow than usual, it could have been a room in any expensive hotel. A rich carpet covered the floor, velvet curtains hung at the windows. An ornate bed built against one wall was covered by a satin bedspread with an evening gown spread across it, and a plump chair stood on gilt legs beside a mahogany dressing-table. Pulling aside a curtain, Rowan peered out at the countryside racing past the window to reassure herself that she was still a passenger on board a train. Sinking slowly into the over-upholstered chair, she stared at her reflection in the mirror.

Before she could do more than remove her hat, the door opened to admit the tall figure of the maid.

"I've put a gown out ready for you, miss," she said, indicating the bed. "I chose the cream satin — cream is the Countess's favourite colour."

Rowan looked at her. "I am not the Countess," she said coldly. "And while we are alone I shall not pretend to be. What else is there?"

For once Helga was flustered. "Well . . . naturally they're all what would have pleased her," she said. "I chose them with her taste in mind, that's what the captain said to do."

Sighing, Rowan stood up and opening the wardrobe door, examined its contents; the only other possible choice was a pale apricot silk, with ribbon bows forming tiny sleeves and a low neckline. Instantly falling in love with it, she drew it out and, holding the heavy folds against her, turned to view herself in the mirror. One glance was enough to convince her that she and the absent Countess had likes in common and, abandoning her stand without compunction, she announced that she would wear it.

"It's not exactly to Countess Clara's taste," said Helga doubtfully. "I only bought it because it was the right size and style. It wouldn't be her first choice."

Already Rowan was out of her travelling dress, the velvet skirt and bodice a crumpled heap on the floor. "Help me," she said, impatiently, struggling with the apricot folds and, reluctantly, the maid hooked her into the dress.

When Helga had dressed her hair and had clasped a row of gleaming pearls round her neck, Rowan eased on a long pair of cream gloves and regarded her reflection with excited delight. A woman equally as attractive as any she had seen at Hillington House gazed back at her, her eyes wide with pleasure and her lips parted in surprise. Above the low-cut bodice her shoulders felt exposed and cold in the unaccustomed air, while her bosom rose and fell with the agitation of her breathing.

"You look a picture, miss — a real beauty," the maid's voice trailed away uncertainly as she added. "And — not overmuch like the Countess, after all."

Carl Von Holstein rose at her entrance, turning to greet her, a glass in his hand. As his eyes fell on her he was momentarily still, taking in her appearance with obvious admiration.

"Tonight I am Rowan Winter," Rowan told him, rustling forward. "Tomorrow I will be your Countess."

"Miss Winter — the pleasure is mine,"

the soldier declared, kissing her fingers gallantly and leading her to the white damask-covered table set with elegant silver.

Feeling more like an actress in a play than herself Rowan accepted soup and fish, followed by roast duck and a cold lemon dessert. By the usual standards of gargantuan meals, it was not large or elaborate, but cooked with flare and served with care, it brought home to the girl how different to her usual circle was the society into which she was about to move. Disquieting thoughts and worries entered her head, but she put them all aside, determined to enjoy this evening whatever the morrow might hold.

Von Holstein filled her glass and watched with amusement her reaction to the white, sparkling wine. The unfamiliar alcohol brought a glowing colour to her cheeks and animation to her manner; to his interested gaze she seemed to become more attractive each moment and less like his cousin.

"I have only drunk champagne once before," she confided.

"And do you like it?"

"Very much — it reminds me of the elderflower wine my father's housekeeper used to make."

"I think you will find it not so innocuous as that innocent country drink — if you drink it in company, when you are the Countess Clara, you must take care what you say."

"I will — I will," she promised airily, chagrined to have the Countess mentioned and defiantly drained her glass.

The soldier smiled, well aware of the reason behind her action. "That is the last time I shall mention Clara," he promised. "Tonight you are the delightful Miss Rowan Winter and I am your attentive escort."

Helga and a manservant entered and quietly cleared the table, while Rowan and the hussar retired to a high-backed couch below one of the windows. After filling her glass, the German pushed a box of chocolates towards her, lighting a cigar, he leaned back as he drew on it, eyeing her appreciatively.

"Have many told you that you are beautiful?" he asked at last.

Rowan shot him a startled look. "No one," she told him honestly, laughing a little at the astonishing thought.

"How very remiss of them," continued Von Holstein. "And one which I intend to rectify with all dispatch. Miss Winter — you are lovely. In that dress you remind me of a butterfly who has crept out of her drab chrysalis to surprise the world with her beauty."

Rowan twisted the long stem of her glass, staring down at the swirling liquid. "Anyone could be beautiful in a gown like this," she said quietly. "If I put on my blue serge skirt and white blouse I should become a plain, dull governess again. Without these trappings of splendour you would find me of little interest, Captain Von Holstein."

There was a hint of bitterness in her voice as she spoke and more than a shade of defiance in her eyes as she lifted her chin to stare challengingly at him.

"What a poor estimate you have of me," said her companion softly. "But I take leave to doubt that you will become a plain dull governess again — or that you ever were. Plain — well, you did subdue your looks to suit your trade, but having sampled the joys of admiration I don't think you will forgo them willingly. As for dull — " he shook his head slightly. "Not in a million years could you be dull, my *liebling Fräulein*."

Rowan gazed at him, suddenly overwhelmingly aware of his charm, warned by some instinct to beware of the frank caress in his voice. As if by chance his arm rested along the couch behind her, his hand lightly touching her bare shoulder, and she shivered slightly at the feel of his fingers against her skin.

"Do you think Helga could bring my wrap?" she asked, sitting up straighter. "I'm feeling a little chilly."

"Of course," he said smoothly and rang the bell for the maid, meeting her at the door and giving her instructions in a voice too low for Rowan to hear. She returned quickly with the satin wrap and, taking it from her, Captain Von Holstein placed about Rowan's shoulders, his hands lingering in a touch more intimate than she liked.

"I have sent Helga to bed," he said. "She really looked very tired and there is no reason for her to wait for us."

Rowan's head came up. "There is every reason," she answered quickly. "If she is my maid, not only have I need of her services, but I should have the ordering of her whereabouts." Lifting her chin, she faced him steadily, her eyes sparkling with anger. "I shall have need of her shortly," she said, with meaning. He raised his eyebrows and stroking his upper lip, fell to watching her through lowered lids, his eyes a pale gleam.

"I have no intention of being seduced, you know," she told him conversationally and flicking open her fan, waved the cold air against her hot cheeks with an assumption of calm she was far from feeling.

"So forthright," he marvelled. "Such British phlegm."

To her surprise he returned to his seat beside her and removed the fan from her startled grasp. "When I choose to seduce you, Miss Winter, I assure you, you will not protest," he said, as she turned a wide-eyed gaze upon him. "This may have seemed like a seduction scene to your bourgeois mind, but, in reality, it was merely a little trial run . . . in anticipation, so to speak."

While he spoke he touched the bow of her dress and then ran his fingers lightly across her shoulder, with a touch so delicate that it could have been a moth's wing that brushed her skin. A shiver of anticipation ran down her spine and, with a smile at her reaction to his caress, he cupped her chin in his hand, holding her prisoner while he leaned close.

"Don't fight me, *Liebchen*," he said softly, his breath fanning her cheek. "We are kindred spirits, you and I, and could deal well together."

Rowan looked at him thoughtfully. "But only consider the difficulties . . . I am sure that the Von Holsteins would object to such a plebeian wife for one of their noble family," she said, practically and had the satisfaction of seeing the smile leave his face and a frown take its place.

"You misunderstand me, madam," he said. "It was not marriage I had in mind."

"Oh — you meant an alliance," she answered in an artless tone. "I wouldn't care for the uncertainty, you see — and then of course there would be the children — "

There was a stunned silence from her companion and then a sound like the ghost of a chuckle.

"You never cease to surprise me, Miss Winter."

She raised her eyebrows at him. "Because I speak frankly? Of course I know how the aristocracy behave — I assure you that opera dancers and *demi-mondes* are commonplace conversation in the servant's hall." For a moment longer she looked at him, letting him read the scorn she felt. "I must decline your offer, Captain, I find I have no wish for a brief glorious hour and then to be married to your head groom or the estate plumber when you tire of me."

"I see you have no good opinion of me," was Carl Von Holstein's rueful comment.

"Oh, not only you, sir. Pray don't feel I single you out," she answered cheerfully and, when he rose abruptly and went to fill his glass, before leaning against the far window and gazing at her with an abstracted air, she knew that all danger of attempted seduction was past and allowed herself to relax a little.

"I find I have quite a liking for travel," she said lightly when the silence had grown uncomfortable. "Of course the luxury of one's own carriage is not often to be sampled and one which I do not suppose I shall enjoy again, but I fear I have the taste for far-flung places and doubtless shall apply for a position abroad when — "

"Don't prattle, Miss Winter," he told her abruptly. "Pray do not belittle your intelligence — or mine." She looked a question at him and he smiled tightly. "I am very well aware of the means you employed to remove a situation you did not care for. I am sorry that you found my attentions so unattractive. Accept my apologies and be sure that bother you I will not again."

Shaken pride made his accent more noticeable than usual and he appeared very foreign and unapproachable as he escorted Rowan back to her room. Glancing up at his aquiline profile as he opened the door for her, she was struck by his remote expression and the air of proud arrogance which he had drawn about him like a cloak.

"*Guten Nacht, Fräulein,*" he said, bowing punctiliously and, turning on the words, was gone, leaving her to gaze after his straight back.

Sighing, she went into her bedroom, dropping the wrap on the floor, while warring emotions shook her; not even to herself would she admit that Carl Von Holstein was the most attractive man she had ever met and that to have surrendered to his attentions would have been very pleasant . . . if not at all sensible.

# 5

AS the train pulled into the tiny village of Drachendorf, Rowan stood at a window, eager to see her new surroundings, her heart beneath the tight velvet bodice beating quickly with excitement and anticipation; for now she must assume the role of the Countess Clara and here would be her first test.

Almost imperceptibly the engine drew to a halt, only the faintest of jolts proclaiming the end of the journey as the driver finally applied his brakes. A touch on Rowan's arm captured her attention and she turned from the window to find the hussar beside her.

"Are you ready, Countess?" he asked, his use of the title reminding her of the part she was to play.

Nodding coolly, she placed the tips of the fingers on the arm he proffered and allowed herself to be led to the door.

"Old Braun, the *Bürgermeister*, is waiting to meet you. He's the stout fellow with the bushy white side-whiskers. You should greet him by name, and inquire after his health — but formerly. Smile graciously to the others, they will not expect more."

A group of people in peasant costume was waiting, the women in full skirts, their snowy white blouses half hidden by tight black bodices. Black hats rather like bowlers, decorated with red pompoms, were set straight on their neatly plaited fair hair. The men wore black breeches and jackets, decorated with braid and wide-brimmed hats, with a long feather tucked into the band. Watching the train expectantly, a flutter of anticipation stirred them as the figure in blue appeared in the doorway and the *Bürgermeister* stepped forward importantly to bow low over her gloved hand. Bursting into a flood of German, so thickly accented that she had difficulty understanding him, he welcomed Rowan to Drachendorf.

"Thank you, *Bürgermeister Braun*," she replied when at last he fell silent, and looked at her expectantly. "How are you and your family?"

Overcome with emotion, he thanked

her volubly for her interest and launched into an account of the health of several females until Captain Von Holstein cut him short with a smile.

"Another time, Braun," he said pleasantly. "At the moment the Countess is a little tired from the journey."

Rowan smiled graciously and a little later waved her hand from the window of the carriage as they drove off. Leaning back against the padded seat, she gazed out at the wooden houses with their carved, sharp gables as they drove through the village. Children stared and pointed, until cuffed into suitably respectful attitudes by their mothers, while the adults bowed or curtsyed gravely as the little cortège passed. Smiling and nodding, Rowan and her companion acknowledged their salutes, relaxing only when the last of the houses was behind them and the empty road stretching ahead between rows of tall pine trees.

"You did very well," said Carl Von Holstein quietly.

"It wasn't difficult," she told him, "but other times will be. Surely some of the servants will have known the Countess Clara since she was a child — how can I hope to deceive them?"

The soldier looked at her, an unfathomable expression in his eyes. "Servants are not paid to notice," he said with a return of his former arrogance. "They will know better than to comment or even think upon anything about the family. I do assure you."

Chilled by his words and the implication of total power behind them, Rowan lowered her lashes and stared at her gloved hands, with a renewal of the apprehension she had formerly felt. As though sensing her unease, Carl Von Holstein left the subject and began telling her about the castle and its locality.

"Of course, with your knowledge of German, you will know that *Drachen* means dragon and the story is that somewhere in the hills above Drachendorf is a cave where a dragon sleeps, ready to wake at any disturbance and terrorise the valley once again."

"Again?" queried Rowan, interested despite herself.

"As he did before — until my ancestor

fought him and, winning the battle, banished him to the hills."

"Very romantic," she commented dryly.

"As all good fairytales should be."

"For a moment I thought you believed it — "

"Some of the local folk do — we have a holiday to celebrate his banishment, when people come into Drachendorf from the surrounding district and everyone enjoys themselves. You will like it — we dress in peasant costume and go incognito. The villagers pretend not to recognise us and take liberties which they usually would not dream of — I expect you will be kissed by the youths and I shall be waylaid by the boldest village maidens. The day ends with a feast and a dance in the courtyard of the castle."

The road steepened and, leaving the shelter of the forest, began to climb upwards, until, the carriage rounding a rocky crag, Rowan caught sight of a castle perched high above them.

"Drachenschloss," announced Carl Von Holstein, a note of pride in his voice, which made Rowan steal a quick glance at him before returning her attention to the building they were approaching.

There seemed to be a profusion of turrets and crenellated walls of varying heights all peering over one another in a confusion of grey stone and narrow windows; the overall impression was of an illustration to one of the more frightening of the fairytales of the Brothers Grimm.

With a clatter of hooves the carriage swept under a tall gatehouse and into a cobbled courtyard surrounded by high walls. It halted beside a flight of steps which led up to the massive door of the castle, and the hussar turned to Rowan.

"Welcome to Drachenschloss, Countess," he said and kissed her hand as the door of the coach was opened by a servant in green breeches and jacket trimmed with leather, made in the same style as that of the villagers who had met the train.

As she made to descend, Von Holstein put out a detaining hand, holding her elbow. "We are not familiar with the servants," he said. "I should have told you earlier. They efface themselves and we ignore them."

Although she had heard of much the same attitude among the nobility of

England, Rowan was barely able to restrain the shocked dismay she felt. Stealing a surreptitious glance at the manservant as he helped her descend she found he kept his eyes lowered and seemed as impervious to her as the captain was to him; although so near, they might have inhabited totally separate worlds. Chilled by such an unnatural situation, she allowed Von Holstein to lead her up the steps and into the castle, where an elderly man, who by his manner and dress could only be a butler, awaited them.

"Welcome, welcome," he said, bowing low, and Rowan was relieved to see a smile appear on her companion's face.

"Kuper, you old rogue," he said, clapping the frail shoulder. "I am pleased to see you."

"The Count thought the new butler in need of a holiday. I am to be here for the rest of the summer," the old man said meaningly.

"You remember Kuper, my dear Clara," said the captain, turning to Rowan. "He was here when we were children — the Von Holstein's oldest and most trusted retainer, in fact."

"Of course," smiled Rowan, following his lead. "I hope you are well, Kuper."

The butler bowed again. "I hope my daughter has looked after you properly, my lady."

After hesitating for only a moment, Rowan realised that he was referring to Helga and at once could see the family likeness shared by the gaunt old man and tall severe woman. "Helga has looked after me very well!" she assured him.

The old man nodded. "She's a good girl," he said with satisfaction, "and absolutely loyal."

"Y-yes," she agreed doubtfully, not sure if she was being warned or reassured.

"I am sure the Countess is tired," put in Carl and, once again, she was aware of how watchful of her he was, and how he smoothed and eased her way.

"Of course," said Kuper and gestured to someone hidden in the far shadows of the cavernous hall. "Mitti is new since you were here last, my lady," he said quietly as a young girl in a dirndl skirt and embroidered blouse came forward.

The words were for her alone and

whereas before she had suspected that he was aware of the conspiracy, now she was convinced of his knowledge and involvement.

"The Count is away for a few days," he went on, escorting her to the foot of the stairs. "He was sorry not to be here to greet you, but will return as soon as possible."

"Do you know where Count Otto is?" asked Carl easily, and Rowan paused to hear the answer.

"I believe he was invited to visit the Dowager Empress, Captain Von Holstein," came the butler's voice, and Rowan went on her way, thinking that the Count's visit was obviously to do with the possible choice of his sister as a royal bride.

As the wide stairs climbed higher and left the sombre hall below, they gave way to an encircling gallery lined with enormous paintings, dark with age. Glancing over the banisters, Rowan looked down on the chequered floor and saw Carl Von Holstein and the butler deep in conversation. Proud, painted faces gazed out of their frames as she passed, reminding her forcibly, with their blonde hair and arrogant stare of the only other Von Holstein she knew. Avoiding their cool grey eyes, she hurried after Mitti's full skirts and found herself in a wide corridor that led into a more modern part of the castle.

Here, dark wood-panelling gave way to flowered wallpaper, and ancient polished floorboards to thick blue carpet. Mitti opened a door and stood back for her to enter.

Pausing on the threshold, Rowan almost gave an exclamation of pleasure as she took in the bright, sunlit room, but recalling that Clara would be well acquainted with the turquoise furnishings and gilt furniture, she managed to control her delight, and say calmly that she was glad to be home.

"We're all pleased to have you, miss — my lady," said the girl, dropping a curtsy and blushing rosily at her own temerity.

"Have you been here long?" Rowan asked, pulling off her gloves and going to look out of one of the full-length windows that filled one wall.

"My grandfather settled in Drachendorf years ago when he was a young man. My mother keeps house for him and I've been at home with her until now."

"And do you like it at the Schloss?" asked Rowan kindly.

"Oh, yes, miss — my lady," cried the girl, pushing back one thick golden plait that had fallen over her shoulder. "All the girls want to work here. It's my ambition to be a lady's maid — "

She broke off as Helga entered, followed by several menservants carrying various boxes and trunks. The older woman shot the girl a quick glance, her brows drawing together in annoyance, and made a gesture for her to go.

"I should like Mitti to stay — I am sure she can help you," Rowan said clearly, turning to the mirror and removing her hat.

"But, my lady — " Helga began, uncertainly.

Holding her eyes in the looking-glass, Rowan sent her a clear challenge. "In fact I should like her to work for me always. I am sure it can be arranged."

Helga's mouth tightened as she hesitated,

unwilling to force an issue in the hearing of the other servants, but well aware that Rowan's move would not carry her employer's approval.

"I shall speak to my brother, the Count, as soon as he returns," went on Rowan easily, "and in the meantime Mitti can assist you to unpack. I am sure you will find her a great help."

Unwillingly, the other woman acquiesced, her sharp tones as she addressed the young girl showing her disapproval. Smiling to herself at having won a battle with the formidable maid, Rowan returned to the window, gazing at the scene below her with fascination; while her first view of Drachenschloss had presented a grim picture of a fortress stronghold, this new angle resembled the colourful, gentle side of a fairy story. Lush trees and thick hedges bounded colourful flower gardens, while the castle seemed to extend at all sides in a mass of buildings of various ages and sizes, ranging from the relatively modern four-storeyed pile in which she was situated to a small prison-like affair directly opposite. Only a formal rose garden separated her from

116

the curious building secure behind its own stone wall, the only entrance to which was by a stout wooden door.

Some air of secrecy about the building attracted her attention and she examined the shuttered windows and firmly closed door with interest.

"What's the building opposite?" she felt impelled to ask, forgetting Mitti's presence and that the girl might be curious at her ignorance.

Helga came to stand beside her. "Have you forgotten, that's where your aunt is kept."

"Kept?" Rowan turned to face her.

With a glance over her shoulder at the oblivious Mitti, who was busy in the inner dressing-room happily putting away the contents of the trunks and boxes, she moved nearer Rowan, speaking confidentially.

"Madam is a little difficult — if you understand. She imagines things and is happiest confined to her familiar surroundings. Everyday life upsets her. She is not at all violent — but to meet her unexpectedly can be disturbing . . . every great family has one such relative — "

"Dear me, poor thing," said Rowan glancing at the sombre building opposite. "Does she never come out?"

"No," she was told uncompromisingly. "You must not think her unhappy or ill-treated. She is well looked after. I merely tell you so that you will not be disturbed by any comings and goings opposite. Sometimes Madam remembers things as they were years ago and becomes nervous and upset. Then the family physician calls to calm her."

Something about the fullness of the explanation bothered Rowan and she found herself wondering why she had been told so much when she would have been satisfied with a briefer reason.

"I see," she said non-committally, feigning uninterest. But later that night, long after the inmates of the castle were in bed, she was brought from a light sleep by a faint noise below her window and was immediately awake and alert.

Sliding out of bed, she caught up the silk wrapper from the coverlet and hurried to the window, her bare feet noiseless on the thick carpet. A gentle breeze stirred the long curtains at the

118

open window, while the silver light from the moon bathed the entire scene in black and white. At first she thought she must have dreamed the sound that had woken her, but, as she watched, a shadow moved and a dark figure appeared against the door of the wall below, the moonlight shining on the familiar blond head. Silently the door opened and Von Holstein was joined by a similar figure, enveloped in a voluminous cloak. He bowed formally, the click of his heels carrying clearly to the watcher above, and then bent his head to kiss the hand presented to him. The woman touched his hair and laughed lightly, the unexpected sound floating up to Rowan on the clear night air, before tucking her hand into his arm. They then left the rose garden and vanished from view, their heads in intimate proximity.

Nibbling her finger, Rowan stared thoughtfully across the intervening walls and roofs to the towering mountains, thinking there had been something extremely un-aunt like about the mysterious figure, even allowing for the fact that her mental faculties were not of the best. Suddenly cold, she shivered, becoming aware of the chill breeze against her arms and shoulders. Huddling into bed, she dragged the covers close about her neck, snuggling down into the comfort. The enveloping warmth soon lulled her into sleep and she awoke to bright sunlight, wondering if she had dreamed the whole episode.

As soon as she decently could she made her way down to the rose garden ostensibly to admire the profusion of blooms, but in reality to inspect the stout wooden door that she had seen open the previous night. Casually, she sauntered nearer, twirling the lace parasol that guarded her complexion from the rays of the sun, pausing now and then to inspect a spectacular blossom. The heavy scent filled her nostrils, while the drone from the myriads of busy bees almost obliterated all other sounds; which was why she was unaware of Captain Von Holstein's approach, or that he had watched her for some time.

"You make a pretty picture, Clara," he said, rousing her from her thoughtful reverie and making her start guiltily, "but tell me what interests you so much in that old door?"

Rowan coloured in confusion. "You should have told me about your mad aunt," she said coldly, determined not to be intimidated.

Von Holstein looked at her. "Tante Marie is not mad — a little eccentric, perhaps, but no more."

"Helga says that she lives here — " Turning, she indicated the stone building behind and looked inquiringly at her companion.

"Just so — "

"Would it not be expected that her niece should pay her a visit?"

"The inmates of the Schloss are used to her ways. She is totally involved in gardening; it would not surprise them at all to know that you had not paid her a visit."

Rowan bent to sniff a rose. "It seems a little discourteous," she commented, careful to hide her interest but inwardly certain that she had stumbled upon some mystery.

"Tante Marie would not expect it — in fact I am certain she would be more than a little surprised, if she remembered having a niece." Bending his head, he spoke confidentially. "Remember you are Clara, Miss Winter, and Clara, I am sure, would have been too busy to take an interest in an elderly, eccentric aunt."

Rowan thought that she was beginning not to care for the Countess, but asked aloud what she would have been doing.

"Riding — every day." Carl Von Holstein broke off to gaze at her in consternation. "You can ride?"

"You should have asked me before, Captain," she said and was pleased to see the anxiety in his eyes.

"Carl — call me Carl. We are cousins, remember," she was told absently, as the soldier gave his attention to the unexpected snag. "You could sprain your ankle, I suppose, if you really cannot ride," he said doubtfully.

"I did not say that," Rowan said calmly, moving away to continue her inspection of the rosebed, tilting her parasol as if by accident between herself and her companion.

The ivory handle was removed from her grasp, the sunshade closed with a force that did the delicate fabric little good and the parasol returned to her. "Miss Winter — " began the hussar forcibly.

"Clara," put in Rowan, "remember we are cousins."

Carl Von Holstein gritted his teeth and took a step nearer so that she had to tilt her head to look up at him. "Be careful, Miss Winter," he warned, "or I will exercise a cousinly prerogative and put you over my knee."

Rowan considered his threat and shook her head. "Now, that I take leave to doubt. You Germans are much too formal for such horseplay, especially with a countess." She eyed the tall, angry figure speculatively. "Now, if I were a servant or a peasant girl — "

"You had best remember, Miss Winter, that I know your true position. An English 'miss,' I believe, would be on a par with either a servant or one of the peasants. Believe me, an attack on your person is not beyond the realms of possibility."

His voice held such quiet menace that Rowan felt a tinge of fear, so small as to be almost enjoyable but which none the less made her catch her breath and lose a shade of colour. While the two antagonists faced each other, the stormy moment was interrupted by the excited arrival of Helga.

"Oh, miss — my lady, the Count is here." Hastily dropping a curtsy as she recalled the masquerade, she continued more calmly. "An outrider has just arrived to say that Count Otto will be here within minutes."

Made nervous by the unexpected event, Rowan turned to Carl for guidance and at once he took her arm.

"We shall meet him," he said.

"My lady, your hair — your dress. And your sunshade closed. How hot and flushed you look," cried the maid, patting her charge's curls and twitching at the skirt of the lace dress.

Carl surveyed her critically, "You look delightful," he told her, meeting her anxious gaze and something like a smile appearing in his eyes, but before she could be sure, he looked away to dismiss Helga and when he turned back it was only to suggest that they should wait at the castle steps to greet the Count.

Rowan found the next few minutes the most difficult and nerve-racking of her life; the thought of meeting Count Otto filled her with uneasy anticipation. Remembering what she had heard of him, together with his obvious autocratic rule at the *Schloss* made the likelihood of being tossed into a deep dungeon, should she not please, seem quite within the realms of possibility. To her chagrin, she found that the agitation of her heartbeat fluttered the lace of her bodice, while the palms of her hands grew damp with fright. Only by steely self-control did she remain outwardly calm, gazing down the steep valley with what she judged to be a sisterly show of interest.

A sudden thought struck her. "How do I greet him?" she asked in a whisper.

"As you always do, Clara, — with a kiss."

The prospect added to her dismay, but the protest was stilled before she uttered it as, at that moment, a cavalcade of horsemen came into view, looking at that distance and height like a scene from a mediaeval pageant; the only elements lacking were heraldic banners floating in the warm air and the glint of weapons.

Even from so far away she could see that the leader was a man of exceptional size and so, when finally Count Otto rode into the courtyard, dismounted and, flinging his reins to a groom, strode towards the castle entrance, she was somewhat prepared for his height and breadth, but nothing had prepared her for the enormous quality of the man himself. Large he might be, but so great was his presence that even if he had been a small man he would have been noticed in a crowd.

Slowly he climbed the stairs, pulling off his gloves and using the moment to take stock of Rowan. Halting in front of her, he studied her critically for what seemed an age, before at last he nodded.

"*Wunderbar, wunderbar!*" he exclaimed to Carl and, seizing her shoulders, lifted her off her heels and kissed her soundly. "My little *Clarachen*," he declared fondly and enveloped her in a bear-hug that dishevelled her hair and ruffled her carefully cultivated calm.

"You're l-looking well, Otto," she returned, feeling that something was

126

called for from her.

"Never better, never better," he cried and reached past her to swallow Von Holstein's hand in a long and violent shake. "Pleased to see you, Carl, my friend," he said and, with an arm about each of their shoulders, walked between them into the castle.

"Well, I must admit that I never thought you'd do it, when you wrote and proposed your scatterbrained idea," he said, when they were alone, "but you've succeeded beyond my wildest imaginings — and saved our honour. I've just come back from a meeting with the Empress Frederick. She likes the family, accepted a portrait to send to England and intends to honour us with a visit in a few weeks to inspect the merchandise."

"Oh, no," moaned Rowan faintly and sat down abruptly.

"What's wrong with you, gal? Look more like my sister Clara than she does herself. Uncanny, I call it. Sure your mama never visited Germany before you were born?" He twirled his magnificent moustaches.

"Of course not — " began Rowan

127

indignantly, stopping abruptly as half-heard and vaguely remembered remarks of her childhood sprang unbidden into her mind. Deliberately refusing to dwell on them for the time being, she sought desperately for something to fill the blank her denial had left. Well aware that both men were regarding her with puzzled interest, she rushed into conversation, saying the first thing that came into her head.

"You looked like a mediaeval lord and his retinue riding up to the castle just now."

Otto took her remark at its face value and seemed pleased with her, smiling and nodding, but she had an idea that his younger cousin was not so easy to divert, however, for the moment, he seemed content to let the matter bide, merely pointing out that her travels seemed to have improved her education.

"I've never known you interested in history before, my dear Clara," he said, warningly.

"We all change as we grow older," she told him, meeting his gaze with a clear challenge in her own, for she was

128

reluctant to put aside a hobby she both valued and enjoyed.

"Not Clara," said the younger man firmly. "She is interested in fashion, society and riding."

Rowan stared. "And nothing else?"

"Stop squabbling, children," came Count Otto's command, his tone brooking no argument. "Carl is right, Miss whoever-you-are. Clara would not be interested in anything as old and done with as history — however, I feel you may follow your hobby discreetly." He rose to gaze out of the window at the distant hills. "I take it you can ride? Good, we will ride out tomorrow and show you to some of my peasants."

# 6

ROWAN approached the promised ride with the Count with some trepidation, finding to her surprise that the sight of Carl also awaiting her arrival in the grey morning air was strangely comforting.

He smiled reassuringly at her approach and, a moment later, she understood why; two horses were already waiting impatiently beside the Count and his cousin, while a groom led out another animal from the stables. Rowan stared at a huge, glossy black mare, with the delicate hooves of an Arab and the nervous, back pointing ears that proclaimed a difficult disposition.

Sending a silent thanks to the local squire who had let her learn to ride with his own children, Rowan stepped forward confidently.

"Let me see if she remembers me," she said to the groom, taking a lump of sugar from the pocket of her black riding-habit.

By questioning Helga the previous night she had learned the mare's name and murmuring it softly, held out the sugar until the long black head was lowered, soft warm lips brushed the palm of her hand and, as the mare crunched the titbit, she was allowed to smooth and fondle the mobile ears and satin nose.

"Hexe — Hexe," she whispered softly and saw the pricked ears flicker and twist at her voice. "What a thing to call you," she went on. "You're nothing like a witch, are you?" And gradually the mare relaxed until Rowan knew that she had won her confidence, only then did she attempt to mount, flying into the saddle with the aid of the groom.

"I see you have not lost your knack with horses," remarked the Count, approvingly, gathering up his reins and moving off.

"Well done," came Carl's quiet voice. "Clara could not have bettered it. Why did you say you could not ride?"

Rowan was beginning to find the repetition of the absent Clara's name decidedly tedious and answered him with a distinct toss of the head.

"I didn't say I couldn't — I merely

did not say I *could*," she pointed out and, clapping her heels into her mount's sides, was the first to clatter under the arch and out on to the road, but almost at once Count Otto rode past and took the lead.

The glance cast in her direction left Rowan in no doubt that he was one of the men who disliked being overtaken by a woman. Hiding a smile at the thought of the many clashes there must have been between the headstrong Clara and her autocratic brother, she fell back, waiting the opportunity to give her horse its head. Although she had not ridden for some time, she had not forgotten the sensation of power and freedom that being mounted on a strong animal gave and found herself revelling in the movement and rush of cool air.

The little cavalcade left the road and turned across a wide stretch of undulating open countryside. Seeing her chance, Rowan urged Hexe forward and, issuing a challenge, headed towards a distant copse at a wild gallop. Shouts behind, followed by the drumming of hooves told her that her challenge had been taken and, crouching lower, she flattened herself behind her mount's nodding head and cried encouragement in her ear.

The turf flew by underfoot as Hexe lengthened her stride, and the trees approached with astonishing speed. The top hat, which had been perched at a rakish angle, tore free from the anchoring veil and sailed away, leaving her hair to tumble unheeded down her back. Just as she began to draw in her reins preparatory to swerving away from the copse, a thunder of hooves told her that her challenge had been met and the long neck and neat head of a horse appeared on either side of her, boxing her in.

She was turned skilfully and brought to a halt, with a finesse which reminded her of dogs herding sheep. Both men regarded her silently for a moment, then the Count leaned forward to pat her cheek.

"My sister is noted for her horsemanship," he said. "You, my dear imposter, will not disgrace her ability."

He smiled and nodded his satisfaction and, as he rode off, Rowan read the open admiration in his eyes. Turning to Carl, she was met by a very different emotion and saw with surprise that his eyes sparkled dangerously, while his mouth was tight with anger.

"What made you do such a foolish thing? With an untried mount and strange countryside you could have — " He broke off abruptly and flicked his boot with his riding-whip.

He had not said, but his tone clearly implied, that he was furious at the danger to all his carefully-laid plans and Rowan felt her own anger rise.

"You wish me to impersonate the Countess Clara," she said coldly. "Helga told me that she always makes a headlong rush at the first opportunity — I, my dear Carl, was merely doing my best to act as she would have done. Of course I do see how difficult it would be for you to find another substitute for your cousin if I should die in a riding accident, but you really must make up your mind whether you want me to impersonate Clara to the best of my ability or if the safety of your plans is of supreme importance." She smiled sweetly at him. "Which would you have me do — be careful or be

Clara?" she asked.

She was unprepared for his reaction; reaching across, he took her wrist and pulled her nearer, making her lean forward at an uncomfortable angle across Hexe's neck.

"You, Fräulein, are growing too big for your boots," he told her softly. "Since putting on my cousin's clothes you seem to feel you have attained her situation in life. You, Miss Winter, will do as I say — while I, my dear governess, have a very great urge to take you out of sight of the grooms and put my whip about your shoulders."

He looked capable of carrying out his threat and Rowan stared at him. "You w-wouldn't dare," she gasped, enraged to hear how her voice trembled.

"Would I not, so," he replied, for once his accent very much in evidence, clearly showing the depths of his annoyance. His fingers tightened around her wrist as though about to put his words into action, but at that moment Count Otto asked impatiently why they were waiting.

Releasing her arm, Carl threw it back across her knees. "Don't try me too far — remember our servants have been trained to look the other way," he warned, before, leaving her, he cantered after the Count.

Rubbing her wrist, Rowan stared after him, her eyebrows drawn together in a frown of anger, but later as she caught up with the two riders and, passing Carl, drew level with his cousin no one would have thought her in anything but the best of spirits. The Count was pleased to have her company and, as she set out to be amusing and entertaining, the quiet countryside soon echoed to their laughter and gay conversation. Stealing a glance at Carl, who rode in dour silence, Rowan saw that he appeared more interested in his surroundings than in his companions. Presently he fell back and was soon deep in conversation with his groom, seeming unaware of her presence and, re-doubling her efforts, she was gratified to see Count Otto responding to her manner, his moustache bristling happily, while the sunlight gleaming on his golden hair made him resemble even more an enormous god of legend.

"You and I, little imposter," he beamed

delightedly "will get on. I find I like you better than my sister."

She laughed back at him, aware of the picture she made as she sat her mettlesome steed with ease and tilted back her head the better to meet his blue gaze. She had lost the confining net and pins and her hair tumbled about the shoulders of the becoming black riding-habit she wore. The folds of a snowy cravat encircled her throat and, as she put up a hand to tuck in a straying end, she smiled a little, remembering how her image in the mirror that morning had reminded her of a Regency beau, and well aware that the pseudo-masculinity of her costume only served to emphasise her femininity.

Recognising her smile, with its unconscious coquetry the Count responded, urging his horse nearer and eyeing her with obvious admiration. As though by chance his knee touched hers, recalling Rowan to her surroundings and realising that she had encouraged the German nobleman more than she intended or was wise, she dug her heel surreptitiously into the black side of her mount, making her sidle and dance nervously.

On returning from the ride, she found that Helga was absent and only Mitti waiting to help her out of the heavy habit. The little servant-girl declined all knowledge of the older maid's whereabouts and, but for the fact that she had taken a glass of lemonade to the window of her room to catch a breath of cooling air, Rowan would never have known that her maid had visited the mysterious abode opposite.

To her surprise, she saw the door in the wall open silently and Helga slip out, affording a brief glimpse of a bright garden beyond, before the door was closed and locked, the maid dropping the key into the black embroidered reticule she always carried. Thoughtfully, Rowan retired from the window and, when the maid appeared, she was sitting in a chair idly turning the pages of a fashion magazine.

A quick glance told her that the bag was still in her hand. "Ah, Helga," she said, "pray pour me another glass of lemonade." And as she had known she would, the other woman put down the bag in order to take up the jug. Accepting the drink, Rowan asked for the book she had left beside her bed and as the gaunt figure of the maid vanished into the inner room, she was on her feet in a flash. It was the work of a moment to find the key and secrete it in her pocket and, by the time Helga returned, she was once again innocently seated in the chair, with only the suspicion of a hurried breath to betray her action. Watching as the bag was retrieved and carried away, she reflected that it was a pity she had to purloin the key so early in the day, when it would not be safe to use it until after dark and could only hope that its absence would not be noticed.

The rest of the day passed slowly and for the first time since arriving at Drachenschloss Rowan found herself bored and impatient with the life of idle luxury she was leading. Waiting in a fever of impatience until the time would come when she could open the mysterious door, she responded automatically to the Count's pleasantries across the dinner-table, only rousing herself to greater efforts when she caught Carl's speculative gaze upon her.

"I believe dear Clara has overtired herself with her exertions this morning," he remarked as the table was cleared and nuts and wine were placed upon its polished surface.

"I *am* rather weary," she agreed, grateful for the excuse presented, although realising that his intention had not been kind. "How perceptive of you to notice, Carl," she smiled across the table. "I did not know that you had my welfare at heart."

"Only an Amazon could have ridden as you did and not have felt the effects — and you, *liebling*, are obviously very far from that."

His eyes slid over her, lingering on the low neckline of her dinner-gown, before rising insolently to meet her gaze again. With burning cheeks Rowan fought a desire to cover her bare bosom and kept her hands in her lap by an immense effort of will, wishing with all her heart that she had refused to wear the lilac gown as had been her first intention when she saw herself in the long mirror. Against her better judgment she had accepted Helga's assurances and now bitterly regretted the decision which had made her open to the scorn of the man opposite.

"I think it's a very becoming gown," put in the Count's lazy voice, "and no one except a blackguard or a Von Holstein would tell you otherwise." He reached across to take her hand and carry it to his lips with old-fashioned courtesy. "Don't look so mortified, my dear. Rest assured he likes you and is jealous that you like me."

For a moment she stared from one to the other, her eyes flashing indignantly, her breasts rising and falling quickly beneath the offending bodice. "I think you are as bad as each other," she declared frankly, standing up. "I shall leave you to your own devices — "

Chairs scraped across the floor as the men came to their feet.

"Pleasant dreams, little one," smiled Count Otto, remaining in his place.

To her chagrin, Carl escorted her into the hall, lighting the candle for her himself from the ones that were placed ready at the foot of the stairs.

"You can still leave," he said hurriedly. "Give me your word to say nothing and I will see that you catch a train to the coast — "

Rowan looked at him thoughtfully. "I don't want to leave," she said firmly and, taking the candle, began to climb the stairs. Looking back as she turned the corner at the top, she saw him standing where she had left him, his face a pale blur in the gloom. With a curious gesture he raised his hand, letting it drop as he turned away. Rowan listened to the diminishing sound of his footsteps echoing across the tiles of the hall floor before she, too, turned away and hurried to her room.

She rang the bell for Helga to help her undress and, relieved of the tight corset and heavy skirts, wrapped herself in a silk négligeé and, dismissing the maid, went to lean against the window-frame, gazing out at the moonlit garden while waiting for the *Schloss* to settle itself for the night. At last the lights began to go out until every window save her own was dark. From behind her the delicate chimes of a clock proclaimed midnight and Rowan stirred, counting the strokes. After one more glance at the still garden and the quiet castle she left the window, having pulled the curtains so that the lighted room would not betray her movements.

She had already decided upon wearing the blue serge skirt and dark jacket of her governess days and now, slipped them on, struck by the speed with which her body had become unfamiliar with the heavy garments. Creeping downstairs, she found, as she had suspected, that the big main door was locked and bolted, but, turning aside undismayed, she hurried into a small side room and found, as she had hoped, that the long windows there, which gave on to the garden, were easily opened. Stepping out on to the terrace, she pulled the doors to behind her, and paused momentarily before darting across the intervening rose garden, she slid into the shadows of the old wall and made her way quickly to the door. The key turned easily and with a quickly beating heart Rowan pushed open the door and slipped through into the forbidden garden.

Even in the moonlight which drained

everything of its colour she could see that she was in what had once been the lady of the castle's bower. Elegant colonnades and arches edged the wall, framing the paths and beds of the garden, while old, but still delightful, buildings formed the living accommodation of what was a self-contained unit within the *Schloss*.

Expecting to meet Mary of the nursery rhyme, she wandered along the winding paths, pausing to touch a blossom or smell a bloom, lost to all save the wonder and beauty of the moment, until she found herself near an open window, its long curtains stirring slightly in the gentle night air.

Unable to resist her curiosity, Rowan drew near and, pulling back the curtains with one hand, peered in. She saw a daintily furnished bedroom, its carpet and walls snowy white in the moonlight. Under the white counterpane a girl slept, her dark hair a cloud upon the pillow. As she gazed, the sleeper stirred and, suddenly awakened to the impropriety of her actions, Rowan turned and fled, not stopping until she was on the other side of the door, leaning against the rough wood trying to calm her panting breath.

When she awoke the next morning she could hardly believe that her nocturnal adventure had not been a dream, but the key under her pillow soon convinced her of its reality. At first, she resolved to have nothing further to do with the secret garden, but upon the reflection she hid the key in the pocket of her old blue serge skirt, where she could be certain it would not be found in case she might ever have need of it.

The days passed quickly with little to disturb their even tempo; in the mornings she rode, usually with either or both of the cousins, "to show herself off to the peasants," as Count Otto put it. In the evenings they ate in the huge dining-room, interminable meals which left Rowan restless and suffering from indigestion. To her dismay, she found that she began to look forward to the minor skirmishes with Carl Von Holstein as the main happenings of interest in the long summer days. She even began to view the Countess Clara's avid interest in fashion and society in a more kindly light, realising how much the other girl must have needed something to fill her empty days.

Quite suddenly all was changed; she began to have an uneasy feeling of being watched. Several times when she was out with Carl or Count Otto she had the impression of eyes upon her, but finding no cause for her nervousness, tried to dismiss her unease as imagination. Then, one morning when both the Von Holsteins had stayed at the castle upon some business affair, she had dismounted as she always did to lead Hexe across a narrow plank bridge to which the mare had long ago taken exception when a man rushed out of the shelter of some nearby trees and clasped her surprised figure in his arms.

"Clara — Clara!" he cried, pressing ardent kisses to her unresponsive lips. "Where have you been? Why have you not answered my letters?"

Rowan pulled his hair until the pain made him come to his senses and as his hold on her slackened, gave him a smart push and stepped back, her riding-whip raised threateningly.

146

The man stared at her and his arms fell limply to his sides. "You — you're not Clara," he said blankly, his eyes wide with bewilderment in a white face. As though his legs would no longer hold him, he staggered to a tree-stump and sat down, his head in his hands.

Rowan watched him, uncertain what to do; here was an unexpected factor — someone who certainly knew the real Countess and who could be the downfall of all the Von Holstein's careful plans. Something in his attitude of abject despair roused her pity and, knowing the wise action would be to ride on and leave him, she found herself asking who he was.

"Laurence Graves," he told her and, lifting his head, stared anew at her. "Of course I can see now that you are not even really alike — the resemblance is in your build and colouring and a certain type of bone formation." He eyed her almost objectively for a few seconds, momentarily forgetting his misery, as he studied her features with interest.

"You're an artist," said Rowan, who had seen the same professional detachment when Lady Devonish had had her portrait painted.

The man nodded impatiently. "That's how I met Clara — I painted the portrait of her in the hall. But where is she? I *must* see her."

In his agitation he rose and looked so wild that Rowan took a hasty step backwards, wondering if she could reach the mare and mount before he caught her.

"Don't be frightened — I won't hurt you," he said, recognising her fear. "But I must know about Clara. I've watched you for days, waiting for an opportunity to speak . . . and now I find that you are not she — "

He went on. "The castle's impregnable, not even a mouse could get in and not one of the servants will even look at a bribe." He rubbed the back of his hand across his eyes. "I must know where — *how* she is." He looked at Rowan with sudden suspicion, his expression almost fearful. "Why are you masquerading as her? She's not — she *can't* be dead!"

"No." Rowan hastened to reassure him, "but she isn't well and for — for political reasons no one must know."

"I've been so worried," he said and sat down again. "We want to be married and she was hoping to persuade the Count to give his permission. I had to go on a commission to Paris — we thought it would be wise to accept it even though we didn't want to be parted, in case the Count refused his consent and we needed the money. She came here months ago and I haven't heard from her since. At first I thought she was busy but lately I've almost been off my head with worry."

"You don't suppose she might have changed her mind?"

"No," he said simply.

Rowan was impressed by his certainty and found herself warming to his loyalty so that when, sensing her sympathy, he asked her if she knew Clara's whereabouts, she did not simply deny all knowledge.

"Will you let me into the castle?" he asked, pressing home his advantage.

She shook her head. "It's impossible. How could I?" Seeing his return to wretchedness she relented a little. "I might — just *might* be able to give her a message," she told him, and such a wave of relief and hope swept over the artist's face that she prayed that her guess was right and she would not have to disappoint him, for, by this time, her former wariness had turned to sympathy and compassion. "Have you paper and a pencil?"

"Here." Feverishly, he hunted through his pockets and thrust a crumpled envelope at her. "I've had a note ready for days in case the opportunity arose."

She slid the letter into the bodice of her riding-habit and, with his aid, mounted Hexe again. "How shall I find you again?" she asked, gathering up the reins.

"There's a woodman's hut deeper in the forest," he said, indicating backwards with his head. "You can leave a message there if I'm not here."

Riding back to the castle Rowan knew that she was pleased rather than otherwise with the meeting; a little thrill of excitement rose in her at the thought of upsetting Carl Von Holstein's plans. A little thwarting would do that arrogant gentleman a great deal of good, she reflected and could hardly curb her impatience for night to fall so that she could return to the secret garden and its lonely inmate.

One self-appointed task awaited her and, although she had very few doubts as to Laurence Graves's tale, she felt she had to be sure of his authenticity. With this in mind she tossed the reins to a waiting groom and hurried into the great hall of Drachenschloss. Pulling off her riding-gloves she slowly circled the walls, inspecting the many paintings that hung there. At last she came back to where she had started and had to admit that none of the portraits there could, by any stretch of imagination, be of the Countess Clara.

"Are you looking for something?" inquired a voice behind her and turning, she found Carl leaning against the newel post of the staircase.

"I was looking for a portrait — the one painted last year," she said meaningly.

"The one your fellow countryman did, you mean," he replied carelessly. "I believe it's in the blue parlour. My cousin took a dislike to it."

Rowan's heart leaped at his confirmation of the stranger's story. "I'd like to see it."

"Then come with me." He led the way to a little-used part of the castle. "How did you know about it?" he asked opening a door.

"Oh — someone must have mentioned it," she answered, forcing herself to sound casual as she preceded the soldier into the room, stopping abruptly as she caught sight of the picture over the mantelpiece.

"O-h!" she said.

"Pre-cisely," said Carl in an imitation of her tone.

One glance explained why the Count had banished his sister's portrait. Clothed in a rose pink evening dress, her hair a dark cloud against a background of windswept sky, the painting was conventional enough to please anyone, but the artist had painted a picture of a woman in love and so seductive and sensual was her gaze, so bruised with passion her red mouth that the viewer was left in no possible doubt that love had recently been satisfied.

"H-he must be a very good artist,"

commented Rowan, unable to tear her shaken gaze away.

"I believe he considered that his masterpiece," Carl told her, his dry tone causing her to look at him quickly, but his expression, as he gazed up at the painting, seemed to be devoid of anything other than mild interest.

"Do you know his name?" she asked.

"Graves — Laurence Graves," Carl turned to her. "You're an intelligent woman, Rowan. You must realise that he and Clara had an affair. He was given his condé, but like the adventurer he is, refused to accept his marching orders. He has proved most troublesome . . . If you see him, you must tell me."

"I wouldn't know him, would I?" She shrugged with simulated uninterest and turned back to study the painted Clara. "I cannot see how you can hope to pass me off as the Countess — we are nothing alike," she said frankly.

Taking her shoulders, he turned her to face him, comparing her to the portrait above, his gaze lingering on her own face with an intensity that made her flush and drop her own eyes.

"To that," he nodded upwards, "no — nothing," he said, "but in general there is enough likeness to deceive most people. You could be sisters. The first time I saw you I was amazed by the resemblance, but now you seem to be more and more yourself and I find I dislike this masquerade intensely." He leaned closer, holding her eyes with his. "Leave now, Rowan, before it's too late," he urged.

She stared up at him, wondering what was behind this sudden about face, but mistaking the reason behind her silence, he shook her a little impatiently.

"You won't be out of pocket, I promise," he said, "and if you've a taste for travel we could visit the Mediterranean."

Rowan blinked. "We?" she queried.

"Oh, come now, don't act the innocent. You must know how I feel about you. We quarrel most delightfully and, as you intended, I've found your behaviour of the last few days very tantalising. I'm making you an offer, Miss Winter. We, together, to leave here, forget about Countesses and wild schemes and travel in each other's company for as long as is pleasant."

Rowan's mouth opened in a round circle of astonishment, closely followed by growing rage, but again the hussar mistook her reaction.

"I'm inviting you to become my mistress," he went on brutally, thinking she had not understood him.

Rowan's anger exploded in a flash of impulsive action, with one motion, she raised her hand and struck him across the face with the full force of an aim that was used to dealing smash hits with a tennis racket. Surprise made him rock back on his feet, but when she lifted her arm for another blow, it was seized and held in a grip that made her gasp.

"How dare you — oh, how *dare* you!" she cried, struggling to free herself.

"I dare very easily, Fräulein," Carl told her, his eyes glittering above the bright red mark on his cheek. "An alliance with a Von Holstein is not to be disparaged — "

"I wouldn't *marry* you!"

His laugh was cold and unpleasant. "I would not ask you to," he said and jerked her closer to hold her imprisoned in his arms. "You may not be aristocratic, my dear governess, but I find you extremely desirable."

Despite her struggle, his mouth closed over hers, bruising her lips. Crushing her resistance with his strength, he kissed her into submission and when she lay limp and gasping in his embrace, lifted his head at last to look down at her, triumph in his gaze.

"I think you like me a little," he said, his accent very pronounced.

"No! No!" Rowan struggled free and this time he let her go. "I hate and despise you. You are arrogant and proud and try to take what you want without a thought for others." Rubbing the back of her hand across her mouth, she brushed away the tears that were blinding her. "For all your proud birth and your wealth and position, you are cruel and despicable — "

Her voice broke and, covering her face with her hands, she turned and ran from the room, seeking her apartment with the instinct of a wounded animal flying to its lair.

156

# 7

FOR the rest of that day, Rowan, torn between rage and misery, brooded upon means of revenge. Wild, impossible plans were considered and discarded in favour of the one presented to her by a lovesick artist that morning. Considered from all angles she could not better it; she would deliver Laurence Graves's letter to Clara, who must be the sleeping girl in the secret garden, help her to escape and remove herself from the vicinity of Drachenschloss. Nothing could be more appropriate or deadly to the Von Holstein's ambitions.

At first, she had resolved to plead a headache and dine in her room, but, deciding that Carl would laugh at her poor-spiritedness, she put on her most becoming gown and sallied forth to confront him. To her chagrin, she found Count Otto alone, his cousin having decided to dine elsewhere. However, the

Count brightened visibly at her entrance, his gaze taking in her attire, which he seemed to assume was for his benefit, and immediately began to ply Rowan with a flow of gallantries and compliments. It took all her tact and skill to keep him at arm's length, until she could at last escape to her bedroom.

Having dismissed Mitti, she controlled her impatience until the castle had grown quiet and dark and then crept from her bed, dressed in the dark skirt and jacket, and slipped from her room. The light was still glowing under the dining-room door where Count Otto sat alone over his wine, as, moving quietly, she stole across the hall and out of the castle the same way she had used previously.

It took only a few minutes to skirt the flowerbeds and open the door in the wall. The night was heavy and overcast, with dark clouds hiding the moon, but she found she remembered the way she had come before quite well and was soon standing outside the window, gazing in at the white furnishings and a girl in a voluminous négligée brushing her hair before a mirror.

Raising her hand, Rowan tapped quietly on the window pane and the girl looked over her shoulder, her eyes wide and inquiring as she stepped into the room.

"Don't be frightened," said Rowan quickly and saw at once there was no need for reassurance; the gaze from the dark eyes was far from alarmed.

"You must be the English girl, who is masquerading as me," surmised the Countess Clara, studying her appraisingly. "Well — I suppose there is a likeness, but not in those clothes."

Rowan frowned and made an impatient gesture, dismissing her appearance as immaterial. "Did you agree to this scheme?" she demanded, wanting to get the fundamental question over, before she said anything else.

Clara snorted through her nose. "Would I willingly stay here," she gestured at her surroundings, "with only a button-loose aunt for company?" she asked. "My dear brother thinks he's an all-powerful prince from the Middle Ages and can keep me here indefinitely and I, I, my dear miss, am helpless enough to believe him."

She dropped the hairbrush on to the dressing-table and, cupping her chin in her hands, gazed gloomily at her reflection in the mirror.

"I saw the painting of you by Laurence Graves . . . " Rowan saw she had captured the other's interest.

"Naughty, isn't it?" she said, watching her through the looking-glass.

"Expressive," Rowan agreed dryly. For a moment they regarded each other silently. Then, making up her mind, Rowan took the crumpled note from her pocket and held it out. "He's here and sent you this letter," she said simply.

"Here!" the stool toppled with a crash as the Countess sprang to her feet, turning to stare at the other girl, one hand clutching the edges of her négligée.

Rowan was unable to prevent her eyes opening wide in astonishment or to hide the surprise she felt.

Following her gaze the other laughed a little. "Yes, I am *enceinte*," she said. "How inconvenient of me to be having a baby just when I was in the running to become the future Queen of England — but then, you see, I imagined I would be married before now."

Wordlessly, Rowan gave her the letter, waiting quietly until she had read it, while the implications of the unexpected development filled her mind with speculation. At last Clara looked up.

"You are willing to help us? Why?" she asked as Rowan nodded.

"I find — I do not care for my position."

"The Von Holstein's have a propensity for propositioning any attractive female," said the Countess knowledgeably. "You'll help me get away from here?"

"If I can."

"Otto dislikes being thwarted — it could be unpleasant, even dangerous, for you."

Rowan smiled her disbelief, forgetting her previous fears in her desire for vengeance. "I'm not afraid," she answered steadily.

"In that I find you a little foolish — however I shall be grateful for your aid. You can get in touch with Laurence? Then I shall leave everything to him and do as he suggests. I am so cut off in here that I know very little of what is happening in the castle — you could guide him better than I." For a moment longer their eyes held and then for the first time a crack appeared in Countess Clara's calm. She put out a hand. "Do not, I beg you, fail me."

Rowan took her cold fingers in her own warm grasp. "I will do my best," she promised, and a little later took her leave, hurrying through the dark garden, her mind so busy with plans and speculation that she was unmindful of the need for caution and care, stepping out briskly along the gravel path. Deep in her own thoughts, she did not notice the dark figure in the shadows as she closed and locked the garden door behind her. When he spoke she gave a gasp and a startled jump, turning quickly to face him.

"Good evening, Miss Winter," said Carl Von Holstein, lazily coming forward. "Did you enjoy your visit?"

"I — th-thought you were out," she said inconsequently.

"I returned," he told her blandly, "to find my cousin returning from an abortive visit to your rooms. He was surprised not to find you there. Apparently he felt sure you would welcome him. Helga having confided in me the loss of the key, I had a very good notion where to seek you . . . Pray give to me the key."

Instinctively, Rowan thrust her hand holding the key deep into her skirt pocket and, lifting her chin, eyed him defiantly.

"Don't make things difficult," she was told wearily as the soldier stepped nearer, his hand held out.

With some idea of seeking security in her room or even eluding him and escaping from the castle, Rowan spun on her heel preparatory to flight, but at her first movement, Carl sprang forward and caught her, one arm pinioning her against his body, while the other hand dragged her clenched fist out of her pocket.

"Open," he commanded, tightening his own grip on her curled fingers, until she gasped and reluctantly obeyed him. "Good," he said, "now we will go and see the Count."

"So," said Count Otto heavily, turning from his contemplation of the flaming log-fire that did little to relieve the chill of the library, despite the month. He looked Rowan over indifferently as Carl thrust her into a deep armchair, all his bonhomie replaced by smouldering anger, reminding Rowan of Clara's warning.

"So," he repeated, "you have seen my sister."

Rowan wondered at the finality in his voice before realising that, knowing such a secret, she would never be allowed to leave the castle. A thrill of fear shivered down her spine and, to her own astonishment, she found herself stealing a supplicating glance to Carl.

With a discreet tap at the door Helga entered and, crossing the floor without a glance in Rowan's direction, whispered behind her hand to the Count, who nodded and waved her away. "Helga tells me," he said as the door closed quietly behind the black figure of the maid, "that you took a letter to the Countess and promised to give her reply to that damned artist. Where are you meeting him?"

"I'm not," Rowan told him promptly, realising by his tone that no good was intended to Laurence Graves if the Von

Holsteins found out his whereabouts. "He said he'd find me."

"I do not believe you." Leaning back in his chair the Count studied her thoughtfully. Suddenly he rose and tipping up her chin, towered over her. "What a silly little girl you are," he said, almost playfully, "to think you can take on the Von Holsteins. We always win, *Liebchen*. You haven't a hope in Hades of beating us." He looked over her head. "Has she, Carl, my dear fellow?"

"None," answered his cousin, who had not spoken for some time. "Be sensible, Rowan," he went on. "Tell us what we want to know."

Rowan shook her head. "No," she said, firmly disdaining subterfuge.

Strong fingers pinched her cheek, the sudden pain bringing tears to her eyes. "Shall we show her the dungeons, Carl?" he asked, purring menace in his voice. "I believe the rack is still in working order — and if all else fails, the Iron Maiden seems appropriate."

Backing away, Rowan stared from one to the other, unable to believe that such things could even be suggested in these modern times. "Y-you must be joking," she said, faintly.

Count Otto laughed. "Not at all," he said, spacing each word with deliberation. "Tell us, my dear young lady, or I can guarantee that life will become extremely unpleasant for you."

Suddenly Rowan believed his threats and felt a rush of fear that left her cold and panting for breath, while beads of perspiration broke out on her forehead. Growing impatient at her silence the Count took a step towards her, but Carl spoke before he reached her.

"It would be wise to give her the night to think things over," he said quickly. "I am sure that she would be amenable after spending a few hours in the turret tower."

The Count looked up. "The turret tower, eh?" he repeated, evidently amused at the thought. "You may have something there."

"I have an idea where Mr Laurence Graves may be lurking — I'll take a horse and see if I can flush him out at first light, besides . . . Miss Winter might still be of use to us and we don't want her marked in any way."

With a smile that left his eyes cold the Count turned to study Rowan thoughtfully. "You may be right," he agreed. "Take her away and let us see what a night in the tower does for her spirit."

With a nod to his cousin, Carl took her arm in a grip that warned that an attempt to escape would be useless and led her into the hall, pausing to take up a candle before urging her towards a distant corner, lost in thick shadows. A low, wooden door gave on to a narrow spiral staircase, the fan-shaped stone treads worn and difficult.

"Up you go, sweetheart," he said in her ear, as she hesitated. Feeling her resistance, he placed a hand in the small of her back and pushed her through the arched door. Bending his tall back as he followed her, he closed the door behind them and they were alone in the enclosed space, the flickering light from the candle making strange shadows on the rough walls and highlighting the sharp angles of his face as he looked down at her.

"Where are you taking me?" demanded

Rowan, endeavouring to control the tremor in her voice.

Seizing her hand, the hussar started upwards, dragging her after him. Trying to keep her footing and manage her long skirts, Rowan followed him, willy-nilly, the grip on her wrist like a steel band. After going round so many times that she was dizzy they stopped at last and Carl flung open a door.

"The turret room," he announced, holding the candle high and thrusting her forward.

In the dim light Rowan saw a small, circular room with a few pieces of ancient, rickety furniture and a narrow, unpaned window, through which the wind was blowing. Shivering, Rowan turned back to her captor and found him watching her.

"As you may guess, this room has not been used for some time," he said. "Shall I tell you a little of its history? Its occupant was an ancestress of mine, a naughty lady, who, while her husband was busy with the local feuds and wars, amused herself with a wandering musician. Her irate husband had her imprisoned up here, which is where she died — some thirty years later." He flicked a speck of dust from his coat sleeve. "It's supposed to be haunted — but I don't believe in ghosts myself."

"Carl — !" She started forward, a hand outstretched and he paused, one eyebrow lifted quizzically.

"Giving in so easily, my dear?" he wondered. "I thought you'd last longer."

"Please don't leave me here."

"Even you must admit that it's better than the dungeons . . . Very well, tell me where to find the wretched artist and you may spend what's left of the night in your own room."

To his surprise, she shook her head. "I won't tell you where to find Mr Graves," she said steadily, "I hoped that you did not really intend to behave like a robber baron of the Middle Ages — at one time I thought you quite civilised."

"Tell me when that was," he said dangerously, "The night on the train — or when you saw Drachenschloss and realised how we lived?"

Rowan turned away to hide the fact that his harsh supposition had hurt her.

"Do you know that Clara is pregnant?" she asked, staring out at the dark night beyond the unshuttered window.

"Of course."

"Then why not let her marry the man she loves?"

Von Holstein gave an incredulous shout of laughter. "Clara in love with an impecunious artist! My dear Fräulein, you have too romantic an imagination. Can you picture my luxury-loving cousin in a bare garret, surrounded by washing and babies?"

"She seems willing to face it." Rowan turned towards him and went on quietly. "Are you aware that Count Otto is keeping her in the secret garden against her will?"

In the dim light from the candle his expression was unfathomable and she waited hopefully for his reply. He spoke after an almost imperceptible pause.

"I think, Miss Winter, that you are indulging in make-believe," he told her coldly. "I shall return in the morning to see if you have changed your mind. Until then I bid you *auf wiedersehen*."

His face sardonic, he bowed curtly and

left the room. Rowan's eyes widened as she heard the heavy bolt slide into place, but she restrained the impulse to rush across the floor and batter her fists against the thick oak door, only her pride preventing her from calling out. As her eyes grew accustomed to the darkness, she looked about in the dim light from the window and made her way to a couch against one wall. Putting out her hand, she withdrew it quickly with an exclamation of disgust; what had appeared as a velvet cover had proved to be dust so thick and matted that even the wind whistling across the room failed to stir it.

Wrinkling her nose with distaste, she dusted the surface as best she could with her handkerchief and then sat down. The bench was hard and, in spite of the month, the night was cold, made worse by the interminable breeze that blew endlessly through the narrow opening. Despite her discomfort and the succession of emotions that filled her brain, Rowan was worn out by the events of the long evening and fell asleep to awaken some time before dawn to the conviction that her prison was filled with roses. Looking about in the cold grey light, she could find no cause for the heady perfume that hung on the air and, too sleepy to be puzzled, fell asleep again.

Waking again to the full light of day, she was at first bewildered by her unfamiliar surroundings and sat up abruptly before, recalling the happenings of the previous night, she stood up and, after brushing the clinging film of dust from her skirt and jacket, went to the window. Far below, like a child's toy, the gardens and grounds were spread out in neat colourful order, while, almost lost in soft mist, the distant hills and forests resembled the beginnings of a watercolour.

Stamping her feet, she blew on her cold hands and wondered anxiously how long she would be left in the tower and at last, wandered back to the couch, which she could now see was an ancient wooden daybed, carved and ornate. Idly her eyes travelled across the dirty stone floor, stopping in amazement as she identified a pile of loose flotsam, stirred by the playful wind. Bending, she picked up a crisp brown petal and crushed it between her fingers. The elusive perfume of a summer long ago rose to her nostrils and was gone on the instant, leaving her to recall the scent of roses which had woken her during the night.

Opening her hand, she let the wind take the dry fragments. As the last particle was whirled away, the sound of footsteps ascending to her prison came to her ears and, brushing her hands together, she stood up, the better to face who ever was about to enter.

Carl Von Holstein paused, framed in the doorway as he studied her, before entering.

"No need to look so apprehensive, Fräulein," he said. "You are safe from the embraces of the Iron Maiden, for I found the impecunious artist where I thought he might be."

Rowan found her legs were unsteady and sat down abruptly. "Now what — ?" she asked. "Am I free?"

"Foolish miss," he chided, shaking his head. "Matters have become rather complicated since last night. Our grandmother has expressed an urgent desire to see Clara — and naturally we must comply with her wishes."

Rowan looked at him. "How?" she asked wearily, suspecting the answer.

"You, my dear Miss Winter."

"No," she shook her head. "I won't do it for payment and you have no means of making me."

"Now there, I take leave to differ." The soldier took an impatient turn about the room to come back to Rowan and stand over her. "As I said, Laurence Graves is now enjoying our hospitality . . . I rather think you would be unwilling for anything to happen to him."

"I hardly know the man."

"*Liebling*, I know how tender is your heart and how much you'd hate to be the cause of another's . . . discomfort."

"You should write melodramas for the stage or 'blood-and-thunders' for boy's papers," she told him scornfully. He suffered her disparaging gaze impassively and at last she spoke again. "How do I even know that you really have him prisoner? You might very well just be saying so."

He smiled. "How astute of you, Miss

Winter. However, I do assure you that my cousin's some time lover is indeed lodged in one of our second best dungeons. Will you take my word, or would you like to see him?"

Rowan read the truth of his statement in his eyes and sighed. "All right Herr Captain, we are back to square one and I will do what you ask. Though even you cannot really expect your grandmother to take me for Clara."

"*Grossmutter* is blind and very frail. Any visits to her are of necessity of the shortest duration . . . if you do as I tell you she will notice nothing."

Rowan stared up at his bland face, incredulity on her own. "I believe you are totally mad," she declared with conviction.

The German made her a mock bow. "Perhaps you are right," he said indifferently. "And, now, let me escort you to your room, where Helga has prepared a bath to remove last night's ravages."

His eyes travelled over her, not hiding the fact that he found her disarray amusing. Flushing under his gaze, Rowan brushed ineffectually at the dust and cobwebs adhering to her clothes, wiping her grimy hands over her hair, and face, thereby unknowingly transferring a black streak the length of her cheek.

Carl's smile widened and, taking a handkerchief from his pocket, he stepped forward to tilt her chin with one hand. "Let me," he said and rubbed her cheek clean.

Finding his attention more than a little disturbing, Rowan stepped hastily out of his grasp and was chagrined to see by his expression that he was fully aware of her feelings.

"When am I to call upon your grandmother?" she asked from a safe distance.

"We will visit her this afternoon. I shall escort you — to be sure that all goes as arranged."

Surrendering herself to an impassive Helga, Rowan suffered the older woman's ministrations and emerged from her hands, like a butterfly from a chrysalis, with all signs of her ill-spent night removed and in time to lunch off salmon mousse and salad before Carl

176

presented himself at her door.

Raising her eyes from the mirror in which she was watching Helga position the large picture hat, she saw that he was wearing an elegant grey suit, with a cut away jacket and a pearl pin in his pale grey cravat and realised that this visit to the Von Holstein's grandmother was a very formal affair.

Taking in her own pearl pink lace gown and the deeper pink of her hat, he nodded his approval to Helga. "There is just one thing more to make the illusion complete," he said, moving towards the dressing-table and examining the bottles there. "Clara always wears this," he said, selecting a cut-glass container, larger and more ornate than the others and removing the stopper.

Rowan put out a protesting hand. "I do not care — " she began, but before she could say more a liberal amount of ice-cold liquid was splashed onto the base of her throat.

The heavy, cloying perfume filled the air and, exclaiming in disgust, she snatched up a handkerchief and hastily dabbed at the offending trickles, before throwing the sodden scrap of lace back on the dressing-table.

An arm reached past her and retrieved the handkerchief. Calmly availing himself of her wrist, Carl tucked the violently perfumed ball into her sleeve.

"I told you *Grossmutter* is blind — she needs only to smell the familiar perfume to be sure you are Clara. Be sensible, Miss Winter;" he said in a low voice, nipping her wrist a little before finally letting her go.

"It's given me a headache already and I dare say it will make me sick before the afternoon is over," complained Rowan pettishly, gathering up her bag and gloves and accepting a pale pink parasol from the hovering maid.

"Be brave," urged the cause of her troubles, offering her his arm and, even in her anger, Rowan found herself thinking reluctantly, how well they looked together as she caught a glimpse of their reflections in the full-length mirror beside the door.

An open carriage awaited them in the courtyard, the horses and coachman, somnolent in the heat from the afternoon sun. Seating herself Rowan put up her parasol, positioning it to shade her complexion, suddenly pleased with the summer afternoon and her ensemble, which she knew was becoming.

"Very pretty," observed her companion.

Rowan's chin lifted, suspecting amusement in his voice and without disturbing her carefully arranged position, she glanced at him out of the corner of her eye, finding to her surprise that his face was perfectly sincere.

Taking her hand, he carried it to his lips and dropped a light kiss on to her fingers. "My *liebling*, you make a charming picture," he said softly.

Rowan's hand trembled in his. Confused, more agitated than she cared to admit, she found his softened attitude difficult to explain.

"Rowan, Rowan!" he sighed. "Why didn't you take my advice and leave before this charade had gone too far? Now we must play it out — I am as much trapped as you."

"You — are a strange man, Carl Von Holstein," she told him, uncertainly. "I scarcely know what to expect. One moment you are a reasonable person, the next a martinet from the Middle Ages."

"I was brought up to believe that the Holsteins were the élite of the earth . . . that my loyalty was owed solely to the family, that nothing and no one else mattered in the least. And that if one of us betrayed our name, then that person was beyond the pale and deserved neither care nor consideration." He brooded silently, his mouth tight, his eyes hidden behind drooping lashes. "And now, Miss Winter, I find it in me to question such loyalty."

Emboldened, Rowan put a hand lightly on his knee. "Clara is truly in love," she said quietly, thinking she knew the reason behind his disquiet. "She wants to marry her artist. Will you help her to escape from Drachenschloss?"

"I only question my loyalties," Carl said harshly. "You mistake the matter if you think I have totally disowned them."

Shaken by the suppressed violence in his voice, Rowan withdrew her hand abruptly and sat up, turning away to gaze out at the passing countryside.

"We shall be coming into the village shortly," came a voice beside her after a while. "Smile and bow, if you please. The Drachendorf folk like to see their Countess."

Turning her shoulder pointedly, Rowan nevertheless did as she was bidden as they drove through the little village, nodding and waving graciously, feeling for all the world like Queen Victoria.

"Very good — to the manner born," breathed Carl in her ear. "And now we have only Grandmama to overcome."

Rowan looked at him curiously; there had been a distinct hint of reluctance in his tones and she wondered at the reason. Could his grandmother be so formidable a person that her arrogant grandson was afraid of her? Or could it possibly be that he was genuinely fond of her and disliked deceiving her? Meeting her speculative gaze, the soldier straightened his shoulders and settled his top hat more firmly on his blond hair.

"Nearly there," he said and then, clearly on impulse, settled his companion's query. "Rowan, she's old and frail . . . and I am very fond of her. Do your best — I'd hate her to know about this masquerade. She wouldn't understand, or accept, the reason for it. I am afraid she would not think it honourable."

# 8

A MILE or so outside the village of Drachendorf the carriage turned off the road and drove through an elegant gateway, stopping beside a low house, its twin rows of long windows twinkling in the bright sunlight. Masses of pink roses climbed over its cream stucco walls, creating an area of colour amid the expanse of wide parkland in which it stood.

"It's beautiful," breathed Rowan.

"The castle's dower house," explained her companion, helping her to step down from the carriage. "As you see, we care deeply for our dowagers — but don't think it wise to have them too near."

"It's really charming," she agreed, looking round. "I'm sure the Holstein ladies must be very happy here."

A man in black approached them deferentially. "Good afternoon, my lady — Herr Captain — the Dowager is in the rose garden. World you care to join her there?"

"Yes, of course. No need to come with us," said Carl and crooking his arm for her hand, led Rowan around the side of the house.

The sun struck hot after the cool rush of air during the drive and the scent of flowers hung heavily in the lazy afternoon, while bees hummed busily among the flowerbeds.

"My grandmother spends much of her time in the rose garden," Carl told her, as they crossed the lawn. "She created it some years ago and now enjoys the perfume."

They rounded a thick, high hedge and found themselves in an enclosed square; low knee-high hedges edged the paths, while formal arrangements of myriads of rose bushes of all varieties were set between a neat, flat carpet of crazy paving, Rowan preferred the less formal English gardens, but she had to admit that this had its own special charm. In the centre was a fountain and a rose-covered arch under which an old lady sat.

"We are here, *Grossmutter*," called Carl, as she turned her head in their direction. "Clara and I," he added, covering Rowan's hand on his arm with his as her fingers tightened convulsively.

"Come here, both of you," she said, patting the stone bench beside her.

Carl bent and kissed her lined cheek, before carrying her small, mittened hand to his lips. As Rowan hesitated, he gestured her forward and with a quickened heart beat she followed his example.

"Clara?" said the old woman tentatively, putting out her hand to touch Rowan's hair and cheek.

"Your garden is looking at its best," said Carl. "As usual your roses are spectacular."

"It can hardly have altered greatly since you were here last week," his grandmother told him, a hint of asperity in her voice. "I've never known you to take an interest in gardening."

"It must come with age," he said easily. "Maybe it's the first sign of a man's settling down into domesticity."

"If that's the case, it's high time Otto

showed some sign of it . . . I'm tired of hearing of his actress friends and the latest female to be under his protection. It's time he married and produced a family." She turned to Rowan, sightless eyes not quite on her face. "And you, Clara, what do you think of the possibility of becoming Queen of England?" she asked.

"I'm — flattered," Rowan offered, not sure what reaction was expected of her.

The old lady laughed. "You surprise me," she said. "I would have thought that you expected the English Royal Family to be flattered that a Holstein considered an alliance with them."

Rowan looked towards Carl for help, but he merely smiled slightly and remained silent. "I am well aware of a Holstein's true worth, but even w-we have not numbered a queen among us," she said quietly.

The Dowager pursed her lips. "Well, you're not the only one being looked over. They'll want a healthy girl, someone who'll breed well. What's this I hear about you being ill?"

"It was nothing — a trifling indisposition," Rowan told her with a silent apology to the real Clara. "I am quite recovered now."

"Hm," was the old lady's thoughtful comment. "Carl," she commanded abruptly. "Go and tell Else that we are ready for tea."

Her grandson gave her a thoughtful look, but went dutifully, if reluctantly, about the errand.

"Now," said the Dowager, as soon as they were alone. "Who are you, girl?"

"C-Clara," stammered Rowan taken by surprise.

"I'm not in my dotage, miss, even if I am blind. That perfume you've doused yourself with didn't fool me for an instant. Quick, tell me who you are. I seem to remember your voice. I've heard it before — a long time ago."

"Clara is indisposed and I've taken her place so that she will still be considered for the Duke of Clarence's bride," said Rowan, seeing nothing for it but to tell the truth.

"I didn't ask what you and my grandson were doing and why. I asked who you were."

There was a surprised pause before Rowan told her. The old lady caught her breath, one thin hand clutching at her bodice, as she leaned back, gasping for air.

Rowan looked at her distress with concern. "Are you all right?" she asked, taking the frail hand in hers. "Shall I ring for your maid?"

The Dowager shook her head impatiently and drawing a handkerchief from her sleeve began to fan herself with it. "Tell me, Miss Winter, did your mother ever visit Germany?" she asked in a voice only a little above a whisper.

"Yes — she did. Before I was born."

Sitting up, the old lady clutched her hand fiercely, peering into her face as though willing her blank eyes to see. "To have attempted this masquerade you must resemble Clara," she reasoned aloud and waited for her companion to speak.

"Yes. Yes I do."

"Oh, my dear girl." Still holding her hand the Dowager sat back and sighed. "In spite of your impeccable German you are English of course."

188

"Yes, my father was a clergyman in Hampshire."

"And your mother?"

"She died some years ago."

The old lady sighed again. "Poor Isabelle."

Rowan's eyes opened. "How do you know her name?" she asked.

"Because, my dear, she spent a summer here over twenty years ago as nursery governess to Clara."

"How incredible! I knew she had been in Germany, but what a coincidence that she should actually have been here."

The Dowager was silent, lost in her own thoughts, her face pensive. At last she spoke again, her voice soft. "I had another son besides Otto's and Carl's fathers. Hans was younger than the other two, a gentle, dreamy boy." Her voice trailed off and she smiled at her memories before continuing. "Hans and your mother fell in love — just before they were to be married he was killed in a riding accident." Her bald statement hung in the air, but before Rowan could express her sympathy, the old lady turned and put a hand on her knee. "You — could — have been my granddaughter," she said, and even in the stress of the moment Rowan noticed the hesitation, almost an emphasis upon the word 'could'.

"How I wish I were," she cried impulsively, clasping the hand on her knee in both her own.

"Oh, my *Liebling*!" murmured the Dowager, reaching forward blindly and in a moment Rowan was held in a warm and loving embrace. "We must talk of this no more," she told Rowan as she released her a few moments later. "It all happened a long time ago. If she never spoke of it to you, then we must respect her wishes . . . but you and I have a very special relationship. It would please me if you thought of me as your grandmother."

Rowan dropped a kiss on her soft cheek, too astounded by these revelations to do more than turn them over and over in her mind. Before she could think of anything to say, Carl returned, accompanied by a retinue of footmen and maids, bearing all the implements of a meal.

"You see, we follow the English custom

of afternoon tea," said the Dowager, as the table was set up and quickly laid.

"Clara would not have forgotten such an institution of our childhood," put in Carl, with a warning glance at Rowan, and for a moment she wondered if the Dowager would make known her discovery of the deception played on her.

"I grow old," she said calmly after an almost imperceptible pause, and Rowan gathered that the knowledge was to be theirs alone. "Will you pour, Clara?" she went on and then maintained an easy flow of conversation while they drank weak tea and ate rich, elaborate cakes.

Thinking of cucumber sandwiches and fresh fruit and cream, Rowan looked at the confection of chocolate and hazelnuts on her plate and smiled at the Dowager's fond impression that the meal resembled English afternoon tea. The sun was hot and the Dowager's unexpected revelation had destroyed Rowan's appetite and she found herself longing for a glass of cool lemonade and a quiet room in which to think. Taking her part in the conversation automatically, she was somewhat surprised to suddenly discover that Carl was on his feet and the visit obviously over.

"Goodbye, *Grossmutter*," she said softly, bending over the little figure.

Tremulous hands reached up and touched her cheek, like the fluttering caress of a butterfly. "*Wiedersehen*, Granddaughter," she said.

Carl looked up sharply but said nothing until they were in the carriage and driving out of the gates.

"She's never called Clara that before," he said.

Rowan continued to gaze out at the countryside. "Granddaughter?" she asked calmly. "How odd. Surely she must have done."

"No — she and Clara do not get on."

Rowan shrugged. "I thought her a delightful person."

"She certainly seemed to take to you," he said slowly. "Which is unusual; *Grossmutter* usually dislikes meeting strangers."

"But, then, I'm not a stranger — I'm her granddaughter." Rowan pointed out, aware of the double ambiguity of her statement.

Carl decided to change the subject. "Did you see our ghost last night?" he asked lazily, leaning back and half closing his eyes the better to study her face.

"No. No grey ladies or knights in clanking armour — nothing save dust and cobwebs."

"Poor rose lady, she must have been very lonely in her tower."

Rowan started uneasily. "Why do you call her that?"

Under the grey jacket Carl's shoulders rose and fell. "That's what everyone calls her. I believe her lover used to bring her roses and the story goes that when she was found, old and dead, there was a single rose in her hand, although it was the depths of winter — Why, what's the matter?" he broke off to ask, noticing her sudden pallor.

Rowan shivered, suddenly cold despite the brilliant sunshine. "I smelt roses and th-there were dried petals on the floor," she told him through stiff lips.

Carl stared at her, his pale gaze startled and incredulous for a moment, before he smiled and shook his head. "You are joking — pulling my leg, *hein*? Someone told you the story before."

Rowan shook her head. "No — I really smelt roses and I had never heard about the rose lady."

Leaning back against the sun-warmed leather, he whistled between his teeth, surveying her thoughtfully. "Well, well," he said quietly. "Maybe there is something in the old legend, after all." Suddenly he leaned forward and covered her hand with his. "I am — sorry about last night. Otto and I were angry at the downfall of all our plans — we allowed our anger to outweigh our judgment. We should not have subjected you to such treatment. It was not — chivalrous." His voice was stiff.

Rowan's eyes widened at being the recipient of the soldier's apology. "You surprise me," she told him honestly.

"Because I tell you I am sorry?"

"Because you admit to the faintest doubt that a Holstein is always in the right."

A slight smile showed in his eyes. "You affect me most strangely, Rowan Winter.

I must own that until I met you such a thought never entered my head. Only recently has it seemed at all possible that my family is less than perfect."

His expression was warm, more kind than she had ever seen it and she seized the opportunity eagerly. "Please, Carl, go and see Clara — "

Stiffening, his expression altered as he sat up, his eyes cold and shuttered. On the instant the softer personality was gone and the proud aristocrat in his place.

Retaining her grip on his hands as he released her and would have withdrawn them, Rowan held his fingers and shook them in an endeavour to keep his attention.

"Just go and see her," she urged desperately. "No harm would be done and you'd see for yourself that I'm speaking the truth. You owe it to her. She's your cousin and you've said you are fond of her. Would you allow her to be kept a prisoner, unhappy and pining for the man she loves?"

His cold gaze flickered over her face. "Do you really expect me to believe that the Count would treat his sister so?"

"You said yourself that anyone who betrayed the family name was beyond the pale and deserved neither care nor consideration," she reminded him and saw that her words had given him pause.

"We will leave this subject," he said after a while, but in a tone that made her hopeful that she had managed to weaken his belief in the infallibility of his family. "Let us talk of other things," he went on formally, but was saved from searching for a safe topic of conversation by Rowan exclaiming aloud as they re-entered the village to find that wide arches made of evergreen had been erected across the single street and that men were busily engaged in setting up wooden booths and stalls.

"Tomorrow is our festival — do you remember I told you we would be expected to dress like peasants and attend?"

"I had forgotten. What shall I wear?"

He frowned. "Clara must have a dress somewhere — Helga will be sure to know."

Rowan felt a pleasurable thrill of excitement at the prospect, forgetting briefly the puzzle of her mother's visit to Drachenschloss and Clara's more modern affair of the heart, but recalling the Dowager's story and Clara's imprisonment. She hurried into the castle eager to be alone and mull over the thoughts and half-formed plans that filled her brain.

Like the Dowager, she felt that, out of loyalty to her mother, she could not delve into the matter of her parentage too closely, but as she recalled the facts she knew and various, until now, unexplained aspects of her home life, with her melancholy mother and older, quiet and withdrawn father, she could accept that their marriage had been based on necessity rather than love. As for the Countess and her artist, with no knowledge of Laurence Graves's whereabouts save that he was somewhere in the castle and Clara behind the locked door of the walled garden, there seemed very little she could do for the moment except to hope that her words had given Carl food for thought.

In the hope that Carl might prove an ally, she decided to dine with him and his cousin that night and, busy with her own thoughts, allowed Helga to dress her without noticing what she wore. Catching a glimpse of herself as she descended the stairs, she paused in surprise, staring back at her reflection in the full-length mirror with astonished eyes. With her dark hair piled high on her head, a midnight blue gown clinging seductively to every outline of her slim figure, her smooth, pale shoulders emerging from the froth of lace that edged the low-cut bodice with startling contrast she hardly recognised herself.

"Good God," she murmured. "I look like a Gaiety Girl!"

A half smile played around her lips as she regarded herself and, after smoothing her eyebrows with one finger, she continued on her way, rather pleased with her appearance.

"So," said the Count as she appeared in the doorway, "the little counterfeit Countess has decided to join us. We are not such rogues after all, eh?"

Rowan allowed him to slip an arm about her waist as he led her to the table. "Perhaps I have found that I am a rogue, too," she said, and saw Carl's head come up at her ambiguous words, but Otto took her statement at face value and broke into jovial laughter, patting her cheek as she took the chair he held for her.

"Naughty little girl," he chided, shaking a playful finger. "And Carl assured me that you were a staid governess, without an original thought in your mind."

Rowan glanced at the man opposite, who had the grace to appear annoyed with his cousin's disclosure. "Perhaps I had not — then," she said with a hint of malice, "but I have found my new situation stimulating in the extreme. With such guides before me, I could hardly remain staid — and dull. After all, I always told my charges that one learned by example."

Carl's eyebrows drew together. "I think the Fräulein is warning us that she does not approve of our schemes," he said, his gaze cold.

Rowan gave a light laugh. "Who am I to approve or otherwise?" she wondered. "Are we not all pawns in more powerful hands?"

The Count nodded approvingly. "I am

glad to see that you are not one of these 'new women' we hear so much about. Wanting suffrage and thinking themselves as good as men."

"On the contrary," put in his cousin quickly, "I believe that Miss Winter thinks herself every bit as good as anyone else, regardless of sex or rank."

"Is that so?" demanded Otto, turning to look at her.

"In my position it would take a very foolish person to admit to such feelings — I am a prisoner, completely in your power and quite helpless. I can only submit to being a weak, frail woman and throw myself in your chauvinistic chivalry."

Recalling vividly the manner and expression Lady Devonish had used to great effect upon her various swains, Rowan gazed soulfully up at the Count through her lashes, making her eyes limpid pools of womanly innocence, while her gentle smile held a hint of worldly wantonness.

The effect was all she could have wished for: Count Otto was visibly stirred. His generous golden whiskers bristled with interest while his enormous chest swelled alarmingly beneath his black dinner jacket.

"Gracious lady, you may count upon the protection of the Holsteins," he told her. "My honour is at your feet."

"Be careful, Otto — she'll trample on it," warned Carl in sardonic tones.

"Why don't you go to bed, my dear fellow?" suggested his cousin, helping Rowan to a lavish portion of roast duck. "Be nice to him, *Liebling*," he said confidently to Rowan, "he is a little shy and easily hurt."

"I would not have thought it."

"I assume this arrogant, self-confident air to hide my true feelings," Carl told her, his eyes gleaming as he repeated the words she had used to describe him.

"You manage it very well," she said gravely.

"To hide my true self? But then I have an excellent example to follow and I remember someone saying that was the best way to learn."

"I don't understand a word," Otto said into the ensuing silence, impatient at being left out of the conversation. "You

201

know about our festival tomorrow? Good. Rustic pleasures, you know," he smiled across the table at her in a way that in anyone but an aristocrat would have been a leer. "Much fun is had by all. Everyone is incognito, you understand."

Rowan intimated that she understood very well, privately determining to do her best to avoid the Count's attentions. The long, seemingly endless meal wore on, the need to appear happy and compliant making her weary and tired of Count Otto's heavy compliments and roguishly flirtatious manner. At last the table was cleared and, pleading the need to retire early to fortify herself for tomorrow, she was able to escape.

Something made her linger by the door and almost at once the men's voices resumed and she caught the artist's name.

"What of the fellow?" the Count was asking. "Have you made arrangements for his — removal?"

"Yes," came Carl's reply, accompanied by the clink of glass and she could imagine him replenishing his drink as he spoke. "He will be taken in a closed carriage to Hamburg tomorrow night and from there I have arranged for him to be shipped to Argentina."

"That should take care of his aspirations to join the family," Count Otto remarked with obvious satisfaction. "With him out of the way it needs only for Clara to be persuaded to be sensible — "

He went on talking but as a footman entered the hall at that moment Rowan had, reluctantly, to abandon her post by the door.

Bitterly disillusioned by Carl's obvious inclusion in the Count's schemes still, she wandered to a window and gazed blankly out at the moonlit garden, her fingers of their own volition taking a flower from a vase and tearing it to pieces. After their talk that afternoon she had persuaded herself that the hussar had been prepared to consider, if not accept unequivocally, her statement that Clara was being confined against her will; now she was confronted with the knowledge that Carl Von Holstein's kinder manner had been a ruse and that any warmer feelings had been merely assumed to gain her compliance. Suddenly looking down she saw that her busy fingers had reduced the huge yellow daisy to shredded petals and with an exclamation of disgust she hastily dropped the remains and moved away from the window.

Instead of going to her apartment, she went into the garden, determined to try the door in the wall, in the faint hope that it might have been left unlocked. Mindful of the need for secrecy and suspecting that a servant might have been detailed to keep watch on her movements, she walked idly along the terrace and sat on a stone seat, ostensibly enjoying the balmy night air and the peace of the dark garden before, some time later, she made her way cautiously to the door that gave access to Clara's prison.

It was only the work of a few seconds to discover that the door was secure and she was debating her next course of action when she became aware that another odour beside the night-smelling flowers was scenting the air: the pungent smoke of tobacco was wafting towards her and, with a stifled exclamation of dismay, she turned to examine the dark garden behind her.

"A pleasant evening, is it not?" said Carl calmly, stepping out of the enveloping shadows, the glowing tip of his cigar the only point of colour in a black and silver moonlight world. "I assure you that the door is locked," he went on.

"I — thought it would be."

"How astute of you — but, then, one must ask why you came?"

Realising that she was the Countess's only means of help, she bit back the bitter reply on her lips, knowing that if she was to be of any use to the lovers, she must succeed in deluding the Count and his cousin into thinking her compliant and of no danger to their wild scheme.

"The night was too lovely to waste," she answered easily, "so I came out into the garden. I dare say you'll think me foolish or presumptuous, but I suddenly wondered if the Countess was awake and lonely, perhaps longing for another woman to talk to, so — I tried the door, but it was locked."

"By her own choice," put in the soldier quickly.

Shrugging lightly, she moved away. "Well, perhaps you are right, though I find it hard to believe that anyone would shut themselves away."

"Only if that person wanted the masquerade of your substitution to succeed," Carl pointed out evenly, and Rowan allowed herself to be persuaded.

Smiling, she placed a hand lightly on his sleeve. "I own to a little sentimentality," she said. "I am persuaded that the Countess has need of a feminine friendship."

Carl laughed down at her, his teeth gleaming in the moonlight. "Not our Clara," he told her baldly. "Now, if you were a personable young man with wealth and a title, I would agree that she would care for your friendship, but that of another female — " He shook decisively. "Never."

Rowan sighed and let her shoulders droop in dejection. "I had thought to be of some comfort. Under the circumstances."

"Under the circumstances Clara wishes to be left alone," she was told firmly. "But you have no need to feel rejected, both Otto and I would willingly accept your offer."

She looked up at him quickly, but his expression gave no indication of another meaning behind his conventional phrases. Taking his words at their face value, she smiled up at him and accepted prettily his offer to walk her round the scented, moonlit garden.

The castle and its grounds seemed to have taken on a different dimension; the silver light turned the old stronghold into an illustration from a fairy story, touching its walls and turrets with mystery and magic. Glancing about, Rowan could well imagine that they would be confronted on a turn of the path by an ethereal princess or even a goblin. Struck by the timeless nature of the scene, she suddenly realised that she and her companion were only a fraction of the many men and women who had stood together in the same surroundings.

As though aware of her thoughts, Carl turned to her. "We could be the first couple on the earth — or the last," he said abruptly, his hand sliding up her bare arm.

His touch sent a quiver of excitement through her and, involuntarily, she shivered.

"Are you cold?" he asked, drawing her nearer.

Wordlessly she shook her head as his arm slid round her waist. His body felt hard and masculine against her as her head fell back against his arm and his mouth came down on hers. His lips were gentle and tentative, totally unlike the other kisses he had forced on her and she found herself responding in a manner which surprised her. Still cradling her shoulders, his other hand came up to caress her cheek, her hair with a touch that was gossamer light.

Lifting his head, he gazed down at her for a moment, his eyes questioning, before his mouth found hers again, his kiss deepening. Reaching up, Rowan wound her arms about his neck, twisting her fingers in his hair and, feeling her response, Carl grew more demanding, his caresses more passionate.

An owl flew overhead, its shrill cry breaking the atmosphere and awakening Rowan to her danger.

"Carl — Carl. No," she cried, catching his hands and drawing back as she reminded herself that his lovemaking was merely an expedient to keep her obedient to his commands.

"Please, Carl," she breathed, realising dizzily that in another moment she would have surrendered to his will; even now, if he persisted, he could return her to a state of breathless passion. To her surprise, for she was well aware that a man of his experience had no difficulty in knowing when a woman returned his desires, Von Holstein relaxed his embrace and, still holding her but lightly and a little away from him, looked down at her.

"Rowan?" he questioned.

Hiding from the query in his gaze, Rowan laid her head against his black jacket and at once was aware of his heartbeat, almost as quick and erratic as her own. "Please, Carl," was all she could say, while she trembled between his hands like an aspen tree shaken by a breeze.

"Don't be afraid," he said, and for a moment his cheek rested against her hair.

209

Forcing herself to remember his duplicity, Rowan stifled her own response to the gentle caress and broke away before her resolve was shattered. "I must go in," she said breathlessly, shaken by her body's betrayal and the unsuspected force of her own emotions.

"Of course." Gravely, he offered his arm and, as her fingers slid into the crook of his elbow, Rowan was both surprised and gratified to find a slight but definite tremor of his own, betraying the control he was exercising over his own feelings.

They were both silent as they returned to the *Schloss*, painfully aware of each other's nearness, yet enclosed in the turmoil of their own emotions and thoughts. As she started to climb the stairs he took her hand and carried it to his lips.

"You are right — now is not the time," he said looking into her eyes. "But, later, we must talk of this."

Suddenly she could bear no more deceit and pretence. Longing to be open and truthful, she snatched her hand away.

"Oh, pray don't — don't *pretend* — "

she cried, made inarticulate by unhappiness and frustration. Turning on her heels, she bunched up her skirt with no regard for decorum and, after running up the stairs to the privacy of her room, indulged in an orgy of tears without any real knowledge of why she cried, until her pillow was sodden and her face swollen and flushed.

# 9

BY morning she had cried herself into a calmer state of mind and had decided upon her next move. When, Mitti, the young maid, brought her breakfast tray she detained her.

"You're looking very pretty," she told her, buttering a piece of toast, and she earned a bright smile and a quick bob in thanks. "I'm sure you have lots of young men clamouring to take you to the Dragon Festival. Have you one particular sweetheart? I've seen you talking to a handsome footman."

"Hans, milady," said Mitti promptly. "As soon as my father will allow we're getting betrothed."

"I'm sure he's a worthy young man and I am sure that you want all lovers to be as happy as you are." Seeing the girl regarding her with a puzzled, but definitely interested air, Rowan gestured her closer. "Do you know that the Count has one young man locked up in the

212

cellars just because he dared to fall in love with the wrong girl?" she asked, thrillingly, and was rewarded by Mitti's eyes growing round with wonder while her rosy lips pursed into a soft circle.

"Now, you can help those poor lovers, not as lucky as you," she went on.

"H-how?" breathed the little maid, her thick yellow plaits trembling with excitement.

"See if you can find out where he is being kept. Hans might know. And then tell me."

Fright crept into the wide blue eyes and Mitti shook her blonde head. "I daren't," she said. "The Count would kill me."

"Of course he wouldn't," Rowan assured her. "I wouldn't let him and neither would the Captain."

Somewhat reassured, Mitti listened while the older girl expanded her romantic theme, dwelling on the unhappiness of the parted lovers and appealing to the maid's sentimental nature. At last the girl agreed and, flushed and excited by her errand, ran to the door in a hurry to begin.

"Only find out where he is," Rowan whispered urgently as the maid vanished round the door. "*Nothing* more," she raised her voice a little to call after the flying figure, suddenly conscience-stricken in case she had sent the young girl into trouble or even danger.

Containing herself in a fever of impatience, she was immensely glad that Helga was absent, searching out Clara's peasant costume, which had unaccountably been lost since last it was worn. At last, when she had long finished her meal and unable to lie still and had climbed out of bed to wander nervously round the room, Mitti returned, sliding round the door with so secretive an air that it would have aroused suspicion and speculation should anyone have seen her.

"He's in the dungeon under the Turret Tower," she told her, her eyes huge with her own importance. "And," she paused, her bosom swelled up like a pouter pigeon with pride in her achievement. "And the key is hanging on a hook beside the door."

"Well done!" exclaimed Rowan, hiding

her surprise at the other's competence as a conspirator. "How clever you are, Mitti," she said admiringly. "Now, here's a little present for doing so well," and, stifling her conscience at disposing of the Countess's jewellery, she dropped a tiny pearl pendant on a thin chain into the girl's hand and was at once overwhelmed with thanks. "There's just one other thing," she went on, furthering another part of her plan. "I want to play a joke on the Count and Captain Von Holstein. Do you think you could get me one of those hats the married women wear?"

Mitti nodded, her eyes wide with wonder, and Rowan felt some explanation was necessary.

"If I leave here wearing one of these pretty lace caps like you have, then I could change to a hat and no one will recognise me."

Mitti nodded her understanding of the scheme. "But why should you want to?" she asked.

"To play a trick — like hide-and-seek," explained Rowan patiently, uneasily aware of the many questions the girl could ask and hoping she would voice none of them.

She watched in some apprehension as Mitti took a thoughtful breath, but was saved from the need for more explanations by Helga entering at that moment, with a peasant dress over her arm.

"Oh, you've found it — how clever!" Rowan cried, thankful for the diversion.

Helga shook out the full skirt and petticoats. "Not I, my lady," she said. "The Dowager sent this over and thankful I am, for I've no idea where to look for the other one. I felt sure I could put my hands straight on it, but it seems to have vanished. If I believed in fairies, I'd say one of them had taken it."

"Never mind. It doesn't matter now I've one to wear." She held the full skirt against her and admired the embroidery and lace on the blouse. "How kind of Grandmother to send it."

Later, when after lunch she tried it on, she found that it fitted perfectly, from the top of the snowy cap, perched like a lace fan on the back of her head, to the white stockings and stout black shoes. The short skirt showed more of her ankles than would have been thought modest in London, but the tightly laced bodice and brightly embroidered apron were gay and becoming, while the two, thick, dark plaits that hung on her shoulders transformed her from a young lady of fashion into an attractive peasant girl. Well pleased with her appearance, Rowan smiled at her reflection before turning on her heels in a flurry of petticoats and going down to the hall to meet the others.

Both men turned at her appearance and she just had time to notice that they were clad in black breeches and jackets before Otto hurried to the foot of the stairs and, taking her waist between his hands, swung her down the remaining steps.

"What a little rustic beauty," he said jovially and kissed her heartily. "There will be some lovesick swains at the dance tonight, eh, Carl? Stay close to us, *Liebling*. You'll find that we Germans have a liking for a pretty face."

Sweeping her out into the courtyard, he pointed out that she would have to ride pillion behind Carl, as his horse would not take kindly to a passenger. "One of the prices I have to pay," he said, sorrowfully, indicating his size.

Carl mounted and then reached down an arm to her but Otto stepped forward and, before she could do more than suspect his intention, had seized her again and tossed her up on to the seat behind his cousin.

"Otto has taken a liking to you," commented Carl, as she settled her feet on the wooden board and tried to smooth her ruffled feelings as easily as she set her hair and skirts to rights.

"He certainly has a masterful manner," Rowan said with feeling, tucking her hand into his belt as they started off.

Carl laughed. "Most women like it."

"Indeed." Rowan's voice was icy and again she felt her companion shake with amusement, which added to her growing irritation and she could not resist giving the slim back in front of her a poke with a stiffened forefinger.

"Behave," he told her, "or I'll set you down and you'll have to walk to Drachendorf, and who knows what would happen then? You might meet the wolf who eats little girls or even a witch or a gnome or two."

"I think I've already met the wolf," she said demurely.

He half turned to glance over his shoulder. "Otto or me?" he asked with one eyebrow raised.

"Both," she answered promptly. "I've a feeling you tend to hunt together."

"Then beware, little girl. There's a certainty that if one doesn't get you the other will."

A chill tingle that could only be excitement slithered delightfully down Rowan's back and, involuntarily, her fingers closed more tightly over the soldier's belt.

"Does that please you?" he asked.

"Of course not — I find it very arrogant of you to make such an assumption," she said crossly, annoyed that he had sensed her reaction so easily.

"Don't be angry, *Liebchen*, it's a lovely day and I refuse to quarrel with you. Today we shall forget our arguments and be friends. We shall enjoy ourselves like any other folk come to see the festival. Agreed?"

She only hesitated fractionally. "Agreed."

Turning in the saddle, he twisted his neck to look down at her. "If I did not fear your long, pointed finger," he said, grinning wickedly, "I should suggest we sealed our pact with a kiss."

Somewhat to her own surprise, she reached up quickly one hand on his shoulder and dropped a light kiss on his lean cheek.

"There," she said, settling back on her padded seat and speaking with more composure than she felt. "Pax, for the rest of the day."

"Pax," he agreed quietly, the amusement gone from his voice. Briefly he covered her hand on his shoulder with his own and, aware of her heightened colour, Rowan moved out of his line of vision and gazed at the fields and trees as they passed.

The Drachen Festival had already started when they arrived, riding unobtrusively into the village and leaving their horses in the yard of the inn. No one seemed aware of their arrival and, apart from the normal greetings given to fellow villagers, the usual ostentatious deference paid to the Holsteins was happily absent. Count Otto strolled around, clapping the men on the back, kissing all the women and tossing little girls into the air, in an orgy of benevolence, while Rowan and Carl followed more quietly in his wake.

Rowan soon found that any man who greeted her expected a kiss, while Carl was obviously only too happy to dispense the same token to any Drachendorf lady bold enough to hail him.

"Very forward, we Germans," he remarked dryly as they were approached by yet another group.

"And to think I had supposed you to be formal," murmured Rowan, preparing again to smile and kiss and be kissed.

"There's your little maid — Mitti, isn't it?" said Carl some time later. "She seems to be trying to attract your attention."

Rowan looked up and saw the girl, peering out from beside the striped backing of a stall. "I'll go and see what she wants," she said casually and strolled off before Carl could prevent her.

"The hat, milady, I've got it." Mitti whispered triumphantly as she joined her. "I've hidden it under my mother's stall." She nodded to the awning behind her. "It's my granny's. She says she's honoured to give it to you."

"How kind of her. I'm very grateful, tell her." Rowan said. Glancing over her shoulder, she saw that her companions were hidden among the crowd. "Give it to me now and I can put it on later. I'll take great care of it."

"What's that?" demanded Carl, his eyes on the large bag that she carried, as she rejoined him. "Surely that girl, doesn't expect you to tote things for her?"

Smiling at the indignation in his voice, Rowan shook her head. "It's a present from her grandmother," she told him truthfully.

"Oh, well that's different. Let me carry it for you."

"No," she said, hiding the bag behind her full skirts. "It's too precious — besides it's not at all heavy and I can manage." Slipping her hand into his arm, she smiled confidingly. "If you *really* want to do

222

something for me. I've been longing to sample those delicious looking cake slices on the stall over there."

Diverted, he allowed himself to be persuaded to buy some *Linsertorte* and, munching the almond and jam pastry, they wandered on, the bag hanging from Rowan's elbow forgotten for the moment. In the middle of the village a space had been kept clear in front of a perspiring band playing lively dance tunes. Soon Rowan's feet were tapping to the rhythmic bass and Carl looked at her inquiringly.

"Shall we?" he asked, indicating the couples forming a circle.

"I'd love to, but I'm afraid I don't know it."

"It's much the same as your country dances," he said, sweeping her into the ring and soon she was one of the spinning, clapping and foot-stamping dancers.

Flushed with excitement, she enjoyed the feel of Carl's hands on her waist as he swung her into the air and knew a pang of disappointment when the music finished, but before they could leave the floor the band broke into another tune and, as though by arrangement, a girl swooped upon Carl and a young man claimed Rowan, laughing as they bore them away.

Happy but breathless, Rowan made her escape some time later. Mindful of her determination to tell the Dowager the whole story and ask for help for the lovers, she made certain that neither the Count nor his cousin was watching, and slipped away in search of a quiet spot where she could affect her simple disguise. Tucking her thick plaits under the black hat, she jammed it down on her head and peered into the mirror Mitti had had the forethought to provide.

To her surprise, the bowler-like headgear suited her, even the enormous red pompoms that adorned the crown lending a certain amount of dash to the badge of matronhood. Tipping the brim farther over her nose to shade her face, she left her refuge and, certain of not being recognised, set off in the direction of the Dowager's house.

The sun was hot and the way much longer than it had appeared from the comfort of an open carriage, but at last when the sounds of music and

224

merriment had long grown dim behind her, she saw the elegant gates ahead and, despite her tiredness, quickened her pace.

Skirting the house, she went at once to the rose garden and found the old lady there, as she had hoped she would. The Dowager looked up as her foot crunched on the gravel path, a smile of welcome crossing her face as Rowan made herself known.

"Dear child," she said, fondly, stretching a hand towards her. "Come and sit by me. How pleased I am to see you. Did Carl bring you?"

"No, he doesn't know I'm here. I'm supposed to be at the fair."

"My dear!" exclaimed the older woman. "Do you mean you walked — alone and in this heat?"

Rowan laughed a little at the other's shocked tones. "I'm used to walking," she said. "Remember I'm a governess and have no need of a chaperon."

"I dare say — but it doesn't seem right to me."

"I came to thank you for the loan of your costume," went on Rowan, "and to tell you a story . . . and ask for your advice and help."

The old lady was still, poised for a moment before she reached forward and poured lemonade from a jug on a table beside her. "Drink this," she said, "and then tell me what is bothering you."

Obeying her, Rowan drank the refreshing liquid while marshalling her thoughts, beginning her story as she set the empty glass down.

The Dowager was silent when she had finished, her face thoughtful and withdrawn, but not, Rowan was surprised to see, shocked or astonished.

"What an ambitious family I've spawned," she said at last. "Otto always was devious, even as a child he wove his schemes, I remember. And as for Clara — she should have settled down and raised a nursery long ago." She sighed and pulled at her lower lip, shaking her head over the folly of her grandchildren. "Of course I'll do my best to help . . . but my advice would be to leave it to Carl."

"Precisely what I'd say myself."

Rowan jumped to her feet at the unexpected voice and gazed at the tall figure with amazement. "W-what — h-how — " she stammered.

"It was easy enough," he said, impatiently answering her unspoken question. "It only took a little thought to realise that you'd come here. I gather she has told you the whole tale," he went on, giving Rowan no kind glance before turning to his grandmother.

"Not a very edifying story, is it?" she said. "I had no idea that you'd carry your ambitions this far. Otto, of course, has always wanted to further the family ... and you, I suppose, acted from a mistaken loyalty. My son has much to answer for, in the way he brought you all up."

Carl looked at her steadily. "It seemed possible," he said quietly, "and if Clara had been willing and we had succeeded even you would have been pleased and proud to number a queen among the Holsteins."

For a moment Rowan thought the old lady would fly into a rage, but instead she took a deep breath and after a while, nodded.

"Ah, Carl," she said sadly, "how well

you know mankind. And now . . . what? How do we extricate ourselves?"

"Leave that to me," he answered promptly, causing Rowan to stir involuntarily.

"Oh, *Grossmutter*," she cried, "how can you leave poor Clara in such a predicament? She is your granddaughter and deserves better of you than to be left to the mercy of her ruthless brother."

Carl looked at her coldly. "Tell me, miss, how do you know that is my intention? To conclusions you jump too quickly."

Rowan's eyes opened wide as she stared up at his tall figure silhouetted against the afternoon sun. "What else could I suppose?" she asked, bewildered. "You have resisted all my attempts to tell you the truth. You appear to take notice of no one save your own assumptions and your cousin's orders."

"No, there you are wrong. I took so much notice of what you have said recently that last night I went to see Clara. To find that everything is as you tell me and that she has no other wish than to marry her artist and live with him in a garret. I find this surprising in the extreme and doubt very much whether her love will survive the first year in such surroundings. However," he shrugged, "she has the right to choose her own life and no one, not even a Holstein, should keep her a prisoner."

"Why didn't you tell me?" demanded Rowan.

"Why should I? I intend to effect her and Mr Graves's escape under cover of the dance in the courtyard tonight. The less people who know the better. And you, my dear Fräulein, with your escapade, nearly upset the whole plan. If Otto misses you, he will be on his guard and have both his prisoners watched."

Rowan smiled coldly. "If you had taken me into your confidence I wouldn't have felt the need to leave the fair," she told him sweetly.

"No? It seems to me that you'd do precisely what you wanted to, with no regard for the affairs of others. I suppose I should be grateful that you did not take it into your head to go for a swim!"

Rowan's cheeks flamed. "Oh-oh, you

are unfair . . . Besides, it wasn't a swim, I was paddling."

"Well, now you are going straight back to the fair — "

Rowan stamped her foot. "I'm not going anywhere with you!" she cried.

His anger flared to match her own and, without a word, he swooped on her, snatching her up and tossing her over his shoulder like a bundle, as he marched off.

"Let me know what happens," called the Dowager as her grandson stalked out of sight.

The grip on her legs was too tight to permit any movement, but, clenching her fists, Rowan pummelled her captor's straight back with a will.

"Let me go — *let me go!*" she cried between her teeth, threshing about wildly in her efforts to be free.

The only answer she received was a full-bodied slap across the seat of her skirt, which left her smarting and bruised and more angry than ever. Her head was swimming from the effect of her unusual position and by the time Carl set her down with an ungentle thump on the grass she was so giddy that the world gyrated madly round her for several seconds and she closed her eyes abruptly upon so unpleasant a sight. At last she dared to open them cautiously again and, finding her surroundings behaving normally, she sat up and glowered at the tall soldier, who was in the process of untying the reins of a horse from the gatepost.

"If you run away," he said without looking over his shoulder, "I shall take the greatest pleasure in hunting you down."

"I believe you are a sadist," announced Rowan, making a discovery as she tried to set her dress to rights. She had lost her hat somewhere in the Dowager's shrubbery and her plaits were in imminent danger of coming undone.

"I'd certainly enjoy beating you," Carl told her, the unpleasant gleam in his eyes confirming the truth of his statement. "Try me any further, Rowan Winter, and I'll put you across my knee."

Rowan busied herself with taking the lace cap from the bag which had been over her arm all this time and pinning it to her head. At last she could look at the towering soldier with composure. "I'm ready," she said, lifting her chin to meet his eyes steadily.

Unexpectedly, he reached down and, with two hands about her waist, lifted her to her feet. Still holding her, he shook her slightly.

"You'll do as I say? No more fighting me and pitting your wits against mine?"

Rowan looked away. "It would be useless, wouldn't it?" she said quietly, hiding her impotent rage.

He laughed silently. "I've been a fool to trust you an inch, my counterfeit Countess," he said, tossing her up on to the pillion-seat.

Putting all the innocence she knew how to into her smile, Rowan held his gaze, while her hands reached forward for the reins which he had draped over the saddlebow. Just as her fingers closed over the warm leather, other fingers grasped hers in a grip that made her wince.

"Behave, little English miss," Carl said, almost indulgently, and tightened his grasp until her bruised fingers were numb and the reins slid from her grip.

232

Swinging easily into the saddle in front of her, he enjoined her to hold tightly to his belt and set the horse along the road at a speed which soon covered the distance between the house and the village.

Soon music drifted to their ears and then the village came into sight, the stalls still as busy and the dancers and band still as active as when she had left it and for a moment Rowan wondered if she had ever actually been away; looking at the milling throng, it seemed more likely that she had dreamed her visit to the Dowager. Skirting the crowds, Carl left the horse with its companions and, tucking Rowan's arm firmly into his own, slipped back among the pleasure-seekers with an assurance that dared any to think that they had ever been absent.

"Carl, you've enjoyed the company of our little *Clarachen* for long enough. Now it's my turn."

The Count removed her from his cousin's arm and slipped his own round her waist. "Go and flirt with the village girls," he advised and, waving airily to

Carl, turned about and plunged into the crowds.

Well aware of the sardonic gleam in Carl's eye at her predicament, Rowan ignored his gaze as she and the Count walked away. Instead, she turned all her charm on her gratified companion. Soon her arms were full of fairings: a necklace of carved bone flowers, a carved picture-frame of wood, a box of sticky sweets and a doll in national costume.

"And now," announced Count Otto at last, "we will go home and get ready for the grand dance tonight." He beamed down at Rowan, patting her hand fondly. "And you, my little deceiver, shall be the belle of the ball."

By some alchemy of presence, he gathered his entourage about him; Carl emerging from the throngs of revellers and servants appearing with the horses, as if by magic. The late afternoon was somnolent with heat and Rowan found her eyelids drooping drowsily as they made their way slowly up the road back to the *Schloss*. For the first time she was aware of her nationality as visions of fragrant cups of tea danced tantalisingly behind her closed lids. By the time they entered the courtyard it was as much as she could do to stay awake and climbing the stairs to her own apartment was a real effort.

Helga, who had forgone the pleasures of the fair, produced refreshments, smiling slightly at Rowan's surprised pleasure at the sight of dainty cucumber sandwiches and a silver pot of China tea.

"I've noticed you don't care for coffee and rich tortes," she said, complacently. "With no one here to see, I thought I could indulge you,"

"You are very kind."

Helga shot her a shrewd glance, and went on, having abandoned all pretence that the English girl was Clara. "The scheme seems to be working out badly," she said, baldly.

Rowan was not really surprised at her knowledge but, unaware of how much she actually knew, answered cautiously and noncommittally.

The maid sighed. "It's a great pity that the Countess could not find it in her heart to comply with Count Otto's wishes — still he may yet persuade her," she ended more cheerfully, going on as she took the pins out of Rowan's dishevelled hair and began brushing it. "And you, miss, if I may say so, have played your part well, to the manner born."

"I've enjoyed it." Rowan told her, finding to her surprise that she was speaking the truth. Suddenly the thought of leaving the castle filled her with dismay. The late sun filled the room with warmth and light and yet she found herself unaccountably cold and depressed, shivering slightly as Helga drew the heavy hair away from her neck.

"You'll enjoy the ball," said the maid as though aware of her depression. "Count Otto will look after you. He's a kind gentleman and thinks a lot of you."

"But what of Carl?" Rowan found herself thinking silently and realised suddenly that the hussar's approbation mattered to her more than the approval of anyone else.

# 10

THE rest of the early evening had been devoted to the unbidden thought that Helga had roused. With dismay at first and then anger at her own weakness, Rowan forced herself to acknowledge that while she had fought and quarrelled with Carl Von Holstein, she had gradually and unexpectedly fallen in love with him. Her treacherous heart lifted at the very thought of his name and with a moan of anguish she covered her burning cheeks with her hands and gazed, wide-eyed and dismayed at her reflection in the dressing-table mirror as she contemplated the trick fate had played on her. Recalling the number of times she had laughed at tales of lovelorn governesses, she acknowledged bitterly that her reward was more just than any thought of by the writers in penny magazines.

At last, unable to bear inaction a moment longer and thinking that her dilemma might be solved in some way if she saw him, Rowan jumped to her feet and went in search of Carl, hoping that the wild attraction she felt for him, might prove untrue in his actual presence. Mindful that he had neglected to tell of his plans for that evening she armed herself with this as an excuse and knocked at the door to his apartment with far more aplomb than she was feeling.

A manservant answered her knock, his face impassive as he announced her, before retiring discreetly to leave her alone with the soldier, Carl came easily to his feet as she hesitated beside the door. Stubbing out his cigar, he eyed her inquiringly, his eyebrows raised.

"My dear," he said mildly, "even cousins do not visit each other's rooms without causing comment."

Rowan, who had discovered that his presence had far more effect upon her than his mere name, tore her fascinated gaze away from his face and tried to act normally while her heart pounded in her ears and a burning flush seemed to cover her from her toes to her forehead. Her knees felt turned to jelly and her hands shook so much that she was forced to hide them from his sharp gaze by thrusting them among the folds of her skirt.

"My dear Rowan — is something wrong?" he asked, suddenly concerned and came towards her, his hands outstretched.

Fearing the consequences if he touched her, she backed away, shaking her head. "I — I came — " she began, knowing that she had some errand in mind but unable for the moment to recall it.

Carl studied her quizzically. "I'd say that you have either seen a ghost — or have fallen in love," he said.

Rowan's eyes flew to his face, fearing that he already knew her secret feelings, but his expression was only teasing and, sighing with relief she at last remembered a reason she could give for visiting him.

"I came to ask about your plans for tonight," she said, as calmly as she was able. "What do you want me to do?"

"We can do nothing until it is dark and as the dance ends at midnight we shall have about an hour in which to effect the escape and be out of reach of Otto when he discovers that his prisoners have gone. At about eleven I shall release Clara and the artist, having first placed horses to wait at the north gate. Until then I want you to keep Otto happy and engaged while I see to the horses. When I am ready to collect Clara and her paramour I shall ask you to dance and then you must make your way to the gate, where I shall join you. After that Clara is in your especial care."

Rowan waited hopefully, but he was silent, making no comment upon her own future once the castle was left behind, and whereas once she had regarded his suggestion as an insult, now she would almost have welcomed his proposal. Unhappily aware of the ambiguity of her feelings, and the treacherous vulnerability of her heart that waited only some sign of tenderness on Carl Von Holstein's part for her willingly to fall victim to his charms, she sighed and turned to the door.

"We'll talk of your future later," Carl said again, reading her thoughts, his voice somewhat strained.

Thinking she heard only bored duty in his tones, Rowan's back straightened and her head came up proudly.

"I am able to take care of my own affairs," she told him, her own voice clear and cold as she opened the door and stepped out into the corridor.

Carl would have said something more, but as he took a breath, approaching footsteps were heard and, mindful of her already shaken reputation, Rowan hastily walked away.

The castle courtyard when she entered it later that evening was a blaze of light; torches flared from all convenient positions, high on the stone walls and from the basket tops of tall posts stuck in the ground. The carcass of a pig revolved slowly above a huge bonfire at one side, trestle-tables bent beneath the weight of quantities of food and enormous barrels of beer. Already couples were dancing to the music of the band perched on a small platform beside the castle steps, from which vantage-point Count Otto was watching the proceedings with a complacent air.

Turning as Rowan came out of the door, he reached an arm and drew her forward, holding her against his side.

"Every year this pleases me more," he told her, gazing down at the milling throng. "So have my ancestors watched their peasants for hundreds of years and so will my son watch in the years to come."

The arrogant pride in his voice sent a shiver down Rowan's spine and, sending a quick glance up, she received an impression of hooded eyes and a jutting hawklike nose, before the Count looked down and the cruel expression relaxed into a smile.

"You English do not have the same feeling for ancestry and race as we Germans," he remarked quietly and nodded once or twice before, tucking her hand into his arm, he led her down the steps.

More shaken than she cared to admit by the force she had glimpsed, Rowan allowed herself to be led into a dance, nodding and smiling as she met each new partner, while her heart fluttered with the realisation of the extent of the Count's rage if he found out the plot to ruin his plans to advance his family.

At any other time she would have

enjoyed the peasant dance, but now it was all she could do to concentrate on the steps and her partner's labouring attempts at conversation. The evening advanced and with it Rowan's nervous anticipation grew until she felt sure that the wild thudding of her heart against her tight black bodice would betray her.

She had kept surreptitious watch on Carl's blond head all evening as he joined in the revelries, apparently without a care in the world, but suddenly he was nowhere in sight and, anxiously searching the crowd with her eyes, she became aware that he had been missing for some time. After sending a would-be partner for a cool drink, she moved to a position from which she could watch the Count and saw that he was the centre of a laughing, flirtatious group of girls and seemed set for the rest of the evening. Accepting her lemonade with a gracious smile, she, with only half of her mind, made difficult conversation with her partner. The other half was with Carl. At last her tongue-tied companion was rescued by a teasing girl and almost at once Carl was by her side, smiling and bowing as the perspiring band struck up another lively tune.

"Are you ready?" he asked into her hair, as they revolved slowly.

His closeness as she was pressed against his chest, the warmth of his body as she was held in his strong arms, had a decidedly unsettling influence on Rowan and she made an attempt to draw away only to feel his embrace tighten.

"This is a lover's dance," he whispered, bending his head to her ear. "Even the strictest grandmother cannot complain when a young man holds a girl tightly in a dance."

The heavy waltz tempo altered and, almost to her disappointment, Rowan found herself walking beside Carl, parading slowly round until the music slid back into three-time and she was held in his embrace once more.

"Look at me," Carl commanded.

As she involuntarily obeyed him, he dipped his head and his mouth closed over hers. For the space of a few seconds their lips clung together and then he raised his head, holding her eyes with his as he followed the rhythm of the ancient dance and again they fell into a solemn procession.

As they reached the deep shadows of a dark corner of the courtyard his arm tightened about her waist and with scarcely a break in step they slipped out of the ring of dancers and through a narrow doorway that led into the garden.

Their footsteps echoing on the stones of the path, as they hurried without speaking between the flowers and shrubs, taking to the shadows whenever a window spilled light across their way, until they arrived at the north gate. Rowan had never known it to be unlocked but a touch of her companion's hand set it ajar and they slid through the narrow opening.

A whinny of welcome and the jingle of harness led her to where the horses were tethered a few paces distant and, with a murmured word and gentle hands, Rowan moved to soothe them.

"Won't we be missed?" she asked quietly as the soldier turned back towards the door.

"They'll think we have crept away to be alone," he told her, and the reason behind his unexpected kiss became clear.

"You — you cad!" she cried, using a word culled from the more melodramatic novels of her reading and, in her anger, forgetting to keep her voice lowered. "You kissed me just to provide an alibi. You didn't care what — "

A hard hand closed across her mouth, cutting off her words, and she could only glare impotently over it at her captor.

"Now *there*, *Liebchen*, you are quite wrong," he told her quietly, his breath fanning her cheek as he bent over her. "I care very much — Yes, I kissed you to make an alibi if anyone was watching, but I kissed you because I wanted to and I enjoyed it very much. In fact I shall do it again — properly."

Watching her, he withdrew his hand slowly, running his fingers down her bare throat and across her shoulder in a caress that made her catch her breath. In the moonlight her eyes were huge and black as her head fell back against his hand. Of their own accord her arms came up and encircled his neck, her fingers closing in the thick fair hair that gleamed silver against the dark night.

The kiss was long and deep and left them both shaken and wild for more. Carl ran his hands over her body, straining her to him and with an inarticulate murmur Rowan drew his head down to hers as the love she felt overcame her upbringing and all convention.

Pushing aside her blouse, Carl kissed her shoulder and the soft, gentle curve of her breast, his warm lips sending a thrill of exquisite delight through Rowan, that made her cling closer, eager for the touch of his hard masculine body.

Somewhere deep in the castle a clock struck the hour, the strident chimes making them stiffen and draw back from each other, recalled to their surroundings and the need for urgency. One second longer they stole from time, clasping hands at arm's length and gazing into each other's eyes. Enjoining her to stay hidden, Carl tore himself away and was quickly lost to sight among the deep shadows that screened the door to the castle.

To calm her tumultuous thoughts Rowan turned to the horses tethered to a ring in the stone wall and to her delight found Hexe among their number. With a gentle whinny the mare blew softly into her palm and searched her pockets in her hope of a titbit. Thinking to save time, Rowan untied the reins and stood with them clutched in her hand. She had not long to wait; quite soon soft footsteps and the rustle of movement alerted her to the arrival of visitors and first Clara and then her artist and Carl stepped through the narrow doorway.

"Should Clara ride?" asked Rowan, struck by a sudden thought.

The Countess gave a low chuckle. "My dear," she said, "if the choice is between staying here or escaping, I'd ride an elephant if need be." There was a protesting murmur from the man beside her and she turned to him. "Do not fuss, Laurence," she commanded. "Instead, help me to mount if you don't wish Otto to find us."

"Only be careful," entreated the artist, lifting her into the saddle.

"I will," she promised and, leaning forward, kissed him on the lips before settling herself in the saddle.

Seeing her gesture and hearing the very

real love in her voice, Rowan knew that she and Carl had done the best thing possible in aiding their escape from the *Schloss* whatever the outcome might be. Feeling uplifted and happy she turned a smiling face to Carl and found him watching her. Bending, he scooped her up between his hands and set her in Hexe's saddle. Leaning forward, she laid one hand against his cheek, her heart in her eyes as she gazed down at him. Turning his head, he kissed her palm and then gravely folded her fingers over it.

"Keep it safe until you have need of it," he said, with a smile at his folly before turning away to mount his horse. "We'll go through the woods — as quietly as we can — and join the road farther down the hill," he told them.

"Well thought, cousin — what a conspirator you'd make," came Clara's teasing voice as she urged her horse forward and took the lead.

Without hesitation the Countess led the way, not even slackening pace when they reached the darkness of the trees and Rowan realised that the way must be well known and familiar to her. The sounds of revelry from the castle died away behind them and soon all was quiet except for the soft jingle of the bridles and the sounds of the horses' movements. An occasional owl hooted and the undergrowth rustled as a nocturnal animal was startled by their passage.

As they emerged from the trees and joined the road a train blew its whistle mournfully in the distance and, raising himself in his saddle, Carl turned to stare up at the castle perched on the hill behind them; even at that distance it was easy to see that the festival was over and that the villagers were beginning to stream home, the lanterns and lights they carried bobbing and twinkling like glow-worms.

"We must hurry," said Carl and, obeying him, the others followed as he plunged on to the road and set a good pace towards the village. Watching as he cast many a glance over his shoulder, Rowan knew that he was anxious and grew afraid herself.

She had supposed that they must be making for the Dowager's house and so was surprised when they stopped at the tiny station on the outskirts of Drachendorf.

"Carl — you must explain," came the Countess's tired voice and by her tone Rowan knew that she was puzzled too.

"I have arranged for the overnight train to stop here and take on passengers," he told them.

"How clever," approved his cousin.

"If Mr Graves would care to look behind the bench over there, he will find a bag with overnight things provided by *Grossmutter*." He blew a kiss to Clara and tossed a heavy purse into her lap. "I think of everything, you see — even money."

Taking Rowan's bridle he led her a little away from the others. "And this, *Liebchen*, is for you," he said, putting an envelope into her hands.

"A — letter?" she said blankly, while a terrible suspicion settled about her heart.

Carl laughed shakily at her stricken expression. "Oh, no — no. Not that," he cried, cupping her head with one hand and roughly kissing her trembling mouth. "I do not intend to leave you — not for

251

long, that is. I must go back to Otto and explain. How could I leave him, thinking me disloyal to him? I must tell him the reasons behind my action and ask for his understanding."

"Carl — you mustn't," cried Rowan, clutching his jacket with desperate fingers. "Write to him, but come with us now."

Gently, he unclasped her hand. "It would be cowardly — I must face him, my dear, to retain my honour. I must tell him — he must not *learn* what I have done."

"I'm afraid — "

"No need to be, the letter tells you where to wait for me — open it on the train. Now, I must go."

Clasping her to him, he kissed her hungrily and then more gently before releasing her. He then turned his horse, waved briefly to the others, and galloped away.

The Countess looked after him. "Is Carl not coming with us?" she asked, surprised. "I thought that you and he . . . " she paused delicately.

"He'll meet me later — but now he

says he must confront Count Otto and tell him himself."

"God in heaven, the man's a fool! Otto will kill him!"

Rowan stared at her, her eyes wide with fear. "You think — "

"I *know*. I have seen my brother in a rage. It is not pleasant, I can tell you. His anger is uncontrollable and with his size and strength — even so good a fighter as Carl will stand little chance."

The sound of its whistle heralded the train's approach and belching clouds of steam entered the village, the glow from its engine's fire box clearly in view.

"You two, catch the train — I'll go back to the castle," Laurence Graves said suddenly.

He had been so quiet during their hurried conversation that the girls had almost forgotten his presence, now they both turned to him.

"No such thing, my love," Clara said hurriedly. "I have need of you — think of my condition."

"The Countess is right." Rowan agreed, seeing that the offer was very real and unable to imagine what the puny artist could hope to achieve against the huge count. "Besides, it would ruin all Carl's efforts. What use would it all have been, if you present yourself back to the Count? No, *I* shall go."

Clara eyed her thoughtfully. "I shall not try to dissuade you — neither will I permit my Laurence to go, but I think you might possibly have a good chance against Otto's anger. Take my advice and use your wits and your femininity."

The train drew to a halt amid much puffing and noise. Clara climbed determinedly aboard, holding firmly to the artist as though expecting him to make a renewed attempt to play the hero. Turning in the doorway, she smiled her thanks to Rowan as, emitting a sudden cloud of steam, the train started forward.

"Remember his sense of humour," the Countess called above the pandemonium. "If you can make him laugh, you have won!"

Without waiting for the train to pull out of the village, Rowan climbed back into the saddle and started Hexe up the hill towards the castle. Already returning revellers were nearing their houses and she was aware of their startled faces as she passed them on the road. Gradually the groups thinned out until she had passed the last of them and then the road was empty ahead and she could allow the mare to quicken her pace.

The dusty road stretched ahead like a winding white ribbon leading to the *Schloss* perched high above, its towers and pointed turrets silhouetted black against the paler night sky. The stark simplicity of the two-colour scene reminded Rowan of old nightmares as she dashed along, fearful that she would be unable to prevent some terrible disaster.

At last she reached the castle and, relieved to see the huge gates still open, clattered into the courtyard. One glance warned her that something was amiss, for the servants, who should have been either about their business or safe in bed, were gathered together in anxious groups, whispering and peering at the closed door to the castle.

Throwing the reins to a nearby man, Rowan mounted the steps as the servants parted before her, but when she would have pushed open the door, she felt her arm taken.

"The Count has given orders that no one is to enter," the butler told her, curtly with no deference to her supposed rank.

Raising her eyebrows at his insolence, Rowan drew herself up to her full height. "You forget yourself, Kuper," she said sharply in the manner of Clara. Taking advantage of the doubt she saw in his eyes, she shook off his hand and swept past him into the great hall.

She was met by the sound of metal scraping furiously against metal and the astonishing sight of Carl and the Count locked in combat, the thin blades of their swords catching the light from the candles and turning it to blue oil on the shining steel.

The Count gave a roar of rage and shouted without turning his head. "Out! Out! whoever it is."

"What *are* you doing?" cried Rowan, hurrying forward and sounding to her chagrin like a governess who had found her charges intent upon mischief.

"Go away, Rowan," said Carl, without

taking his eyes from his opponent. "This is no place for you."

"Stop it — oh, stop it," she cried, wringing her hands in her distress. "This is 1890 not the Middle Ages."

"Duelling is part of the German tradition — what better way of settling quarrels," Count Otto told her, briefly. "If you stay be prepared to see your lover die."

With a flurry of movement, he lunged forward, beating Carl backward by the force and strength of his blows. One hand pressed to her hammering heart, Rowan watched in horror, almost unable to believe that such a barbaric scene could really be happening. Focusing all their attention on each other, the men ignored her presence as they each sought for the mastery. For all his immense strength the Count was slower than his smaller opponent, who used his speed to keep out of reach of his cousin's weapon, while Count Otto endeavoured to pin the younger man into a corner, where he could use his superior weight to advantage.

Repelled yet fascinated, Rowan crept to

the stairs and, clinging to the banisters, climbed a few steps the better to see the fight. Although she had only a hazy knowledge of duelling she knew enough to suppose, when the Count's sword flashed forward and Carl jerked back, blood appearing like a streak of paint on his cheek, that honour was satisfied and that was the end of the fight. However the Count pressed forward more fiercely than ever, sending Carl stumbling backward, his face suddenly pale as he realised that his formidable cousin's blood lust would not be satisfied by anything so trivial as a scratch.

With growing fear Rowan watched as the lighter man gave ground, obviously tiring beneath the other's furious onslaught. Although a better swordsman than most, Carl was no match for the Count, who was in the grip of a rage which could have befitted a berserk Viking. Once he stumbled to his knees and was only saved from the point of Count Otto's sword by a desperate lunge to one side.

Unable to stand by without taking action, Rowan looked about for means of putting an end to the fight and, finding nothing suitable in which to catch the weapons, considered wildly whether to throw herself between the fighting men. However, one look at their withdrawn, intense faces made her inclined to think that such heroics would pass totally unnoticed and she abandoned the idea. Something at the head of the stairs caught her attention and her eyes widened as a possible plan presented itself to her, beautiful in its stark simplicity.

Without stopping to consider further, Rowan slowly and cautiously began to edge up the stairs, careful not to call attention to herself. At last the tall copper jug, containing a huge arrangement of flowers was within reach and, certain that she was too high among the shadows above their heads to attract their attention, she leaned over the banisters, holding the jug aloft, and waited for the right moment.

Like fighting animals the men circled below, their panting breath carrying clearly to the watching girl. Even to her inexperienced eyes Carl appeared dangerously weary, only determination keeping his exhaustion at bay as he parried his opponent's heavy blows that now lacked all finesse; the Count was merely intent upon beating his enemy.

The duellists warily circled, each seeking an opening, gradually creeping nearer the waiting girl. With bated breath Rowan watched, the jug raised in both hands and, at last, the men were directly below. With a silent prayer she let go, leaning over the banisters to watch the fall of the missile. At the last moment the antagonists became aware of the falling object and, pausing in their battle, gazed upward in puzzled apprehension in the few seconds it took for the jug and its contents to arrive.

To the girl above, water and flowers seemed to explode in a shower of silver streaks and bright flower-heads. When the unexpected vision cleared she saw an astonished Count, festooned in blossoms, gazing blankly upwards with a wet and silent Carl stretched at his feet. Giving a groan of anguish at the outcome of her handiwork, Rowan ran downstairs with the intention of hurling herself upon the bosom of the supine soldier, but her foot skidded in the water and instead she found herself thrown against Otto's broad chest.

Appearing on the verge of an apoplexy, he clasped her to him with a roar of rage, staring down at her with wild, protruding eyes in a violently red face. Closing her eyes with a whimper of fear, Rowan waited her fate. To her surprise nothing happened; instead she seemed to be in suspended animation, her feet some inches above the floor and her head buried in the Count's black jacket. She became aware of a strange movement from the chest against which she was clasped, which grew stronger with each moment, rumbling and shaking until at last a great laugh burst from Otto's throat.

Cautiously opening an eye, Rowan gazed at the face above her, half suspecting that the shock had driven her captor mad, but, following his eyes, realised with relief that the Count's sense of humour had come to her rescue.

A bemused Carl had sat up, clasping a bent and dented jug to his chest and blinking through the drops of water which slowly trickled down his face.

"By thunder, this wench is a wild one," shouted the Count and kissed Rowan soundly before setting her on her feet.

Flying to Carl's side, she knelt beside him, patting him anxiously. "Oh, my love, are you all right?" she asked, wiping his face with her skirt.

"Better than I would have been in another minute," he said for her ears alone, giving her a glance out of surprisingly sharp eyes. "Well, Otto?" he went on looking up at his tall cousin. "Pax?"

The Count seized him under the arms and hoisted him to his feet. "Pax, you young devil," he agreed. "For the moment — just long enough for you to get out of my sight, I'd say. And you've the governess, here, to thank for that."

For a moment his expression grew sombre again and a frown returned between his brows. Stepping forward, Carl presented him with the mistreated jug, bowing his blond head solemnly, and Rowan was relieved to see a twinkle appear again as Otto looked down at his cousin.

"Away with you," he said, giving him

a clap on the shoulder which would have knocked over a smaller man, "before I decide to teach you a real lesson."

Turning abruptly on his heels, he left them without a backward glance. As a door closed behind him, Rowan's hand crept into Carl's.

"Will he ever forgive us?" she asked.

"In time. Otto's not the man to bear malice — but now it would be best if we left the castle before he alters his mind. One fight with my cousin is enough for any man."

Rowan looked at him. "Were you really unconscious?" she wondered.

Carl smiled. "It seemed a good way to end the duel — without loss of honour to anyone." Looking into her eyes, he pulled her against him. "What a clever girl you are, Miss Winter," he told her softly. "I think you saved my life."

"Dear God, I thought I'd killed you!"

"Would you have minded?" he wondered, tipping up her chin the better to read her expression.

"Minded!" she cried with such a wealth of emotion in her voice that Carl gathered her closer and kissed the horror from her mouth.

Rowan would have been contented to stay for ever in his embrace, but gradually they became aware of movements and murmurs around them and, lifting their heads, saw that curiosity had overcome fear and that the servants were gathered in the half opened doorway.

"The Count is in the library." Carl said, looking over Rowan's head. "If you take my advice, Kuper, you'll not disturb him."

"Very good, Herr Captain," said the butler, bowing.

The hussar took Rowan's hand and, tucking it firmly into the crook of his elbow, marched purposefully to the door. "We are leaving — have the goodness to have our things packed and sent to the Metropole, Paris," he said coolly, completely ignoring the shambles of the hall behind him and the fact that he was wet and festooned with traces of petals and leaves, the remains of someone's flower arrangement.

"P-Paris?" questioned Rowan as she was tossed into Hexe's saddle.

Carl looked at her, pausing in the act of gathering up his reins. "Don't you care for the idea? I thought all women chose Paris for their *Flitterwochen*."

"*Flitterwochen?*" echoed Rowan.

"*Leibchen*, if you take to repeating everything I say I shall begin to have doubts about the wisdom of my action."

"What action?" demanded Rowan more loudly than she intended. "I don't even know what a *Flitterwochen* is. It sounds . . . unusual." Her voice trembled a little.

Carl flung back his head and laughed, his teeth gleaming white in the moonlight. "Then let me tell you that your German has been sadly neglected. Every schoolgirl knows that they are the days that fly by after one's marriage. How do you fancy Paris for your honeymoon, Miss Winter?"

Rowan's mouth formed a silent circle of pleasure and a sigh of happiness escaped her.

"I'd like it very much," she told him simply, her heart in her eyes.

The glance they exchanged was long and full of meaning. Carl nodded gravely as though well satisfied, then:

"Let us start our journey," he said soberly and led the way under the arch.

Already the sky to the east was lightening and, looking back over her shoulder, Rowan saw that the grey stone walls of the old castle were touched with pink. She thought someone moved at one of the turret windows; for a moment it seemed as if a hand waved briefly, but when she turned and looked more fully she could see that no one was there.

"We'll be back, won't we?" she asked anxiously, suddenly sorry to leave.

"*Ja* — one day," Carl told her firmly. "But now we have our future to think about."

Leaning across the neck of his horse he kissed her, his lips cool at first and then warm . . . and Rowan forgot about anything except the present and the life together that fate had arranged for them.